"I guess that's my cue to go," Carolina said with a hint of disappointment

Neil gently took hold of her arm. He had no idea what he'd done until he felt the cool fabric of her coat sleeve beneath his fingers.

"What?" She turned.

Neil had always been a man of actions, not words. That the right thing to say should fail him now was no great surprise.

"Stay." He swallowed, took a breath. "Please." He had to explain. Make her understand.

She remained rigid. "Give me one good reason. You've already hurt me once. I can't handle a second time."

He nodded and let go of her arm.

But before she'd moved so much as an inch, he raised his hand to her cheek and cradled it tenderly.

"How about this for a reason?" he said, drawing her toward him.

Dear Reader,

Carolina Sweetwater first appeared on the pages of *Waiting for Baby* (June 2009) and then again in *Taking on Twins* (February 2010). While I felt she was a perfect foil for her cousin Jake and a great friend to her sister, Corrine, it soon became clear to me she needed her own book and her own hero. But who to match her with? Not just any man would do for Carolina, not with her blend of wit, wisdom and tenderhearted vulnerability.

Acting Sheriff Neil Lovitt is very loosely based on a deputy sheriff I read about a few years ago whose personal tragedy touched me deeply. I frequently remembered the man's story and wondered how anyone could go on after losing a loved one under such terrible circumstances. In *The Accidental Sheriff*, Neil has learned to cope in the wake of his own personal tragedy and created a nice, if uneventful, life for him and his young daughter. It takes Carolina, along with the help of his daughter, to teach him how to really live and love again.

I'm so glad my editor, Kathleen Scheibling, let me add a small suspense element to *The Accidental Sheriff*. It made the book that much more fun to write and, I hope, that much more fun for you to read.

Warmest wishes,

Cathy McDavid

The Accidental Sheriff

CATHY MCDAVID

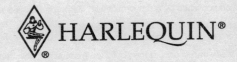

HARLEQUIN®

TORONTO • NEW YORK • LONDON
AMSTERDAM • PARIS • SYDNEY • HAMBURG
STOCKHOLM • ATHENS • TOKYO • MILAN • MADRID
PRAGUE • WARSAW • BUDAPEST • AUCKLAND

Recycling programs
for this product may
not exist in your area.

ISBN-13: 978-0-373-75311-6

THE ACCIDENTAL SHERIFF

Copyright © 2010 by Cathy McDavid.

This edition published by arrangement with Harlequin Books S.A.

For questions and comments about the quality of this book
please contact us at Customer_eCare@Harlequin.ca

® and TM are trademarks of the publisher. Trademarks indicated with
® are registered in the United States Patent and Trademark Office, the
Canadian Trade Marks Office and in other countries.

www.eHarlequin.com

Printed in U.S.A.

ABOUT THE AUTHOR

For the past eleven years Cathy McDavid has been juggling a family, a job and writing, and she's been doing pretty well at it except for the cooking and housecleaning part. Mother of boy-and-girl teenage twins, she manages the near impossible by working every day with her husband of twenty years at their commercial construction company. They survive by not bringing work home and not bringing home to the office. A mutual love of all things Western also helps. Horses and ranch animals have been a part of Cathy's life since she moved to Arizona as a child and asked her mother for riding lessons. She can hardly remember a time when she couldn't walk outside and pet a soft, velvety nose (or beak or snout) whenever the mood struck. You can visit her Web site at www.cathymcdavid.com.

Books by Cathy McDavid

HARLEQUIN AMERICAN ROMANCE

Don't miss any of our special offers. Write to us at the following address for information on our newest releases.

Harlequin Reader Service
U.S.: 3010 Walden Ave., P.O. Box 1325, Buffalo, NY 14269
Canadian: P.O. Box 609, Fort Erie, Ont. L2A 5X3

To Pamela, best friend.
Thank you for all the body parts you've lent me
through the years. An ear to bend when I've just
got to vent, a hand to hold when I'm afraid,
a shoulder to cry on when I'm sad, a foot planted
firmly in my rear end when I need a good kick,
an elbow in the ribs to keep me lined out,
your thumbs up when I've done a good job,
your fresh pair of eyes for critiquing my chapters,
and your big, sweet, generous heart that
you've given me time and again. I love you.

Chapter One

The Marley Brothers Band was loud, but not so loud their music covered the sickening sound of squealing tires, spitting gravel and—here was the bad part—crunching metal.

Carolina Sweetwater whirled around and gasped. The left rear fender of her brand-new PT Cruiser was crushed beneath the front end of a giant, jet-black Hummer.

That wasn't all.

"Briana, are you all right?" she hollered, and hurried toward the two vehicles, mindless of her three-inch spike heels and the yards of taffeta swirling around her ankles.

The Hummer lurched, hissed and then backed slowly away from her car. She reached the Cruiser's driver's-side door at the same moment her niece stepped out.

"Aunt Carolina, I'm so sorry."

"It's all right." Weak with relief, she hugged the shaking teenager and glanced over her shoulder. The occupants of the Hummer were also climbing out and, like her niece, appeared to be unharmed.

"I looked both ways, but I swear I didn't see them."

"What matters most is no one was hurt." Now that Carolina had a chance to catch her breath and assess the situation, she realized the only serious casualty of the minor parking lot collision was her car. The SUV had suffered nothing more than a small scratch or two.

"Are you okay, young lady?" The driver of the SUV, Major Linc Harrison of the U.S. Army, and his wife, whose name momentarily escaped Carolina, approached. He wore a scowl. Her expression was considerably kinder.

"I'm fine," Briana sniffed.

"How about you?" Carolina asked. "Are either of you injured?"

"In that?" The major's wife rolled her eyes at the Hummer. "Hardly."

The major took out his cell phone and punched in a number. "I'm calling nine-one-one."

"Is that necessary?" Carolina tried not to let his precision-cut steel-gray hair and crisp dress uniform, the left side of which was completely covered with medals and ribbons and little colored bars, intimidate her. "Can't we just exchange insurance information and phone numbers? My niece and I would really like to get back to the wedding."

His reply was to lift the phone to his ear and glower at her.

"Dad's going to be really mad, isn't he?"

"He won't be happy." Carolina put an arm around her niece and drew her several feet away to the edge of the parking lot. "This is your second accident since you started driving."

Technically, Briana wasn't Carolina's niece. Her father and Carolina were cousins, which made her and Briana third cousins or cousins once removed or… Calling each other aunt and niece was just a whole lot simpler.

"I'm dead," Briana whimpered.

"You're not dead. Grounded for sure. And you can forget about driving for a while. Like until college."

The teenager burst into fresh tears.

"Come on. I was joking," Carolina said, rubbing Briana's back. "Don't worry. I'll handle your dad. This is partly my fault anyway. I'm the one who let you drive my car." The beautiful, shiny, cobalt-blue convertible she'd bought last month to celebrate her thirty-third birthday.

"Because I asked you if I could."

"And I said yes. Hence, shared responsibility."

In hindsight, Carolina should have driven the five minutes to her cabin and gotten those spare camera batteries herself. Instead, she'd caved when Briana had pleaded with her to run the errand.

The Marley Brothers Band finished their number. After a round of applause, they turned the microphone over to Carolina's older sister Vi. Like the music, every word Vi spoke carried clearly from the lawn in front of the dining hall, over the roof of the main lodge and across the parking lot to where Carolina, her niece, the major and his wife stood. Thanks to the rolling hills, sprawling oaks and towering pines surrounding the main buildings, acoustics at Bear Creek Ranch were great.

"Ladies and gentlemen, friends and family," Vi announced, "please clear the dance floor for the bride and her father."

Carolina cringed. She was going to miss the entire dance— her sister Corrine's glowing face, her father's beaming smile and the besotted expression the groom would be wearing when he cut in to sweep his new wife away from his father-in-law.

Damn! Her throat closed and, for the hundredth time that week, she willed herself to keep it together.

Something about her little sister's wedding had her walking an emotional tightrope. If she didn't know better, she'd think she was envious. Not because of Corrine's new husband, but because of her obvious bliss at being married.

Now, wasn't that a surprise? Who would have guessed avoid-commitment-at-all-costs Carolina Sweetwater harbored a secret longing to find that one right guy she could spend the rest of her life with?

What had triggered the recent change in her thinking? The

wedding? Her birthday? Her bid for better, meatier assignments at work being shot down? The five-year anniversary of
her broken engagement? Definitely the last one. For too long
she'd mourned a man who wasn't worth it.

Carolina needed to get serious if she wanted the kind of
contentment two of her sisters had found. A contentment that
included a wonderful man, a satisfying career and one day
maybe children.

Problem was, the selection of available bachelors between
her family's guest resort in the Matazal Mountains of north-
ern Arizona and the nearby small town of Payson was pretty
slim. Carolina had already dated most of them in an attempt
to convince herself her ex-fiancé hadn't permanently broken
her heart.

"We're really screwed, aren't we?"

Carolina didn't reprimand her niece. In certain circumstances, the term was appropriate, and this definitely counted
as one of them. "We'll be fine. I have ample insurance."

"I think the major's mean," Briana said.

"Not so much mean as by the book."

Bear Creek Ranch had never hosted a U.S. Army major
before. He was her sister Corrine's former commanding officer and had traveled all the way from Fort Bragg in North
Carolina to attend the wedding.

"His wife seems nice," Carolina observed.

As if sensing they were being talked about, the couple
strode over. "How much longer do you think this will take?"
the major groused, checking his watch. A Rolex. "It's almost
six, and we should have been on the road by now."

"Hard to say." Carolina was proud of her well-modulated
voice. She had her part-time job as morning traffic director at
KPKD to thank for that. "The ranch is outside Payson's town
limits. Which means we have to wait for the county sheriff

or one of his deputies. A nonemergency like this could take hours."

The major grunted.

"How about we let my niece go back to the wedding. There's no reason she has to miss out on everything."

He vetoed Carolina's suggestion with an ogre-ish "No. Your niece is in serious trouble, Ms. Sweetwater."

Well, Briana came by it honestly.

Carolina's own free spirit had landed her in hot water on a regular basis since preschool, when she dumped an entire container of fish food into the classroom aquarium and then lied about it. Sometime in grade school she stopped lying, but not landing in hot water. Take today, for example. If there was any way her cousin Jake could manage it, he'd ground *her* along with his daughter.

At the distant rumble of an approaching vehicle, everyone turned in unison. A marked patrol car traveled the long dirt road leading into the ranch and then swung into the parking lot. Carolina craned her neck to catch a glimpse of the driver. Old Sheriff Herberger had a soft spot when it came to her family, who donated regularly to the department's various outreach programs.

Luck, unfortunately, wasn't on her side. It was the much younger, not so kindly Deputy Sheriff Neil Lovitt who stepped from the parked car.

"My, my," the major's wife said, an appreciative hitch in her voice.

Carolina silently seconded the sentiment.

The major's uniform might have sharper pleats and more medals pinned to it, but Deputy Sheriff Lovitt did his own khaki shirt and slacks pretty darn proud. Adjusting his straw cowboy hat and sunglasses, he made his way toward them, his gait casual yet confident, a small notebook in his hand.

"Good afternoon, folks," he said upon reaching them.

Almost two years in this neck of the woods hadn't softened his New York accent one iota.

"Hi." Carolina was the only one who smiled.

Why she bothered, she had no clue. He'd never responded to any of her attempts at friendliness. That included the double date they'd once gone on—ironically, not with each other. Carolina's date worked with Deputy Sheriff Lovitt, which was how they'd wound up going to the community fair together. She'd been far more interested in the deputy than…Mark, was it? Or Alfonso. She wasn't sure. Her attention had been riveted on the department's newest addition.

He hadn't reciprocated her interest, and as far as she could tell, nothing had changed in the time since that disastrous double date.

His loss, Carolina decided.

It was a shame, though. Of all the available prospects in the area, he was the most attractive.

"So, what happened here?" he inquired, his gaze encompassing everyone present.

Briana and the major launched into simultaneous explanations, raising their voices to be heard over each other.

"Enough." Deputy Sheriff Lovitt held up a hand. "You first." He pointed at Briana and put pen to paper, readying to take notes.

The major harrumphed his displeasure.

"I was backing out and…and he…" Briana's nerve seemed to desert her.

"Go on," the deputy sheriff said, his tone encouraging.

"I…he…" She fidgeted.

The major began tapping a very polished boot, staring hard at the cluster of trees on the other side of the parking lot.

"I was being real careful, I swear." Once she started, she couldn't stop. "I checked the rearview mirror and the side mirrors. I didn't even have my foot on the gas pedal. Next thing I knew, this gigantic SUV came from out of nowhere."

"You hit me, young lady," the major boomed.

"That's not true. It was the other way around."

"I was heading toward the exit and you backed out right in front of me." His loud bark caused Briana to wilt.

Carolina fought the urge to step in front of her niece and shield her.

"I had the right-of-way, Officer." The major's already broad chest seemed to swell.

"Deputy."

"Of course," he grumbled. "Excuse me."

"May I see both of your licenses, registrations and proof of insurance, please?"

Carolina went to her car, mourning the damage once again as she passed the bumper. Fetching the necessary paperwork from the glove compartment, she returned to the group, her three-inch heels catching in the uneven asphalt.

Neil removed his sunglasses, dropped them in his shirt pocket and monitored her every move with unconcealed interest.

When had she started thinking of Deputy Sheriff Lovitt by his first name?

Since he couldn't take his to-die-for chocolate-brown eyes off her.

Carolina experienced a small thrill of awareness when she handed him the paper.

"The Chrysler's yours, Ms. Sweetwater?" He said her name without looking down at the registration, which indicated he remembered her from their double date.

She didn't know whether to be flattered or worried.

"Yes."

"Brand-new, I see."

"Fresh off the lot."

"I hope you have a low deductible on your insurance."

"Not low enough." She was already kicking herself for trying to save a few dollars.

Neil skimmed through the major's documents before turning to Briana. "Where's your license?"

"I...ah..."

Carolina had a sinking feeling in the pit of her stomach.

"Miss?" Neil's patience was obviously running low.

"It's a wedding." Briana's shoulders folded in on themselves. "I didn't bring my purse with me."

"Does she need her license?" Carolina jumped to Briana's defense, if only to wipe the satisfied grin off the major's face. "This is private property."

The look Neil shot her could have seared every petal off the wildflowers growing by the road.

Carolina responded by standing taller, which brought his mouth into her direct line of vision. She couldn't help staring at it. After a moment, the corners of his lips, which were really quite nice, started to turn up. Just a little. Hardly noticeable.

Gotcha.

The thought had hardly formed in her head when Jake came charging down the fieldstone walkway toward them. He was accompanied by her uncle and Will, her sister Vi's husband.

"Oh, goodie, here comes the cavalry," she mumbled under her breath, and waited for all hell to break loose.

CAROLINA SWEETWATER TURNED away to face her family. Neil avoided staring at her backside, which was every bit as attractive as her front, a fact that hadn't gone unnoticed when she went to her car to fetch her registration. Her lime-green bridesmaid dress was—well, words couldn't describe it. But Carolina carried the dress off with the poise of a supermodel.

A different time, different circumstances...

"What's going on here?" Jake Tucker, manager of Bear Creek Ranch resort, commanded everyone's attention. "Briana, are you all right?"

"Everyone's fine." Carolina glided to the center of the men, a tropical flower surrounded by penguin suits. Several stray tendrils had escaped the rhinestone clasp holding her hair in place. They lay on her bare neck, the dark brunette color standing out against her lightly tanned skin.

Neil forced his gaze down to his citation book.

"There was a slight fender bender," she said, her voice calm.

He listened to that same voice every morning on KPKD.

"You wrecked your new car?" Jake's voice was anything *but* calm.

"No." Briana visibly braced herself. "I did."

"Your daughter ran into me." The major stepped forward.

Jake closed his eyes and blew out a long breath.

"Please don't be mad."

He shot his daughter a foreboding look. "At the moment, it's hard not to be."

Neil almost felt sorry for her. Almost. He could see his own five-year-old daughter Zoey as a teenager, trembling from head to toe, waiting for the ax to fall. Unfortunately, Briana had been driving without a license and, from what he could determine, had caused the accident. And while it had occurred on private property, the ranch parking lot was accessible to the public.

The choice of whether or not to issue her a citation was Neil's.

Jake listened to an account of the accident and, despite his obvious anger, did an admirable job of maintaining his cool with both his daughter and Carolina. Not that Neil figured she took any guff from her cousin. Or anyone else, for that matter.

"Can my wife and I leave now?" the major asked when Neil was finished taking statements and collecting contact information.

"You folks drive careful," he warned them. "Traffic can be congested this time of day."

"Thank you again for coming to the wedding." Jake shook the major's hand. "I know Corrine really appreciates it."

"I wish we could have stayed longer," the major's wife gushed. "You have a beautiful place."

Neil agreed. The spectacular scenery and quiet country living were the main reasons he'd picked the Payson area in which to settle down. Other than the occasional drunken brawl and dispute between neighbors, not much happened here in the way of crime. Quite a change from Manhattan's Upper West Side, where he'd spent ten years on the force—the last one in a daze, struggling to cope in the wake of his wife's death.

Four years had dulled the pain but not the guilt.

He shouldn't have listened to her, shouldn't have done his duty. Maybe then, she'd still be alive.

Neil retrieved his sunglasses from his breast pocket and put them back on.

"If you need anything, you have my number." The major and his wife returned to their rented SUV after saying goodbye.

"Look, I know the accident was Briana's fault." Carolina moved to stand beside Neil. "But is there any way you can cut her some slack?"

"What are you suggesting, Ms. Sweetwater?"

"A warning?"

"Carolina," Jake interrupted, his tone clearly telling her to butt out.

In truth, Neil *was* inclined to cut Briana a little slack, but not because of her father or Carolina. His instincts told him

Briana was a good kid, if not a good driver. And as scared as she was at this moment, she'd definitely exercise more caution in the future.

"You committed two violations." He ignored everyone else and addressed Briana. "The first was failure to yield the right-of-way, and the second was driving without a valid license."

She nodded resignedly.

"Today—and only today—I'm going to let you off with a warning."

"No way!" Her jaw dropped, and her eyes bugged.

"If I'm called out again to an accident in which you're involved, rest assured I'll throw the book at you."

"I promise. I'll be really, really careful from now on. I'll check both ways three times and never go over thirty miles an hour."

"Just practice reasonable caution." Neil made a few more notes, then wrote up Briana's warning. "That's all I ask."

He received three thank-yous. Briana's was relieved, Jake's appreciative and Carolina's accompanied by a flirty smile.

Oh, boy.

Neil wasn't a recluse. He dated once in a while, but not seriously and not with the intention of remarrying. He liked it that way. From what he'd heard around town about Carolina Sweetwater, she subscribed to a similar philosophy. It should be a perfect match.

But he had no interest in finding that out.

What Neil saw when he looked at her was a woman he wouldn't mind getting to know a whole lot better. And when he linked her name and the idea of remarrying, his stomach didn't turn to stone. For those two reasons, he diligently maintained a safe distance from her. His job was dangerous. It had cost him his wife and his child her mother. He refused to put another person he cared about in danger, the way he had Lynne. Avoiding serious involvements seemed the easiest solution.

"Is that all?" Briana returned his citation book after signing the warning. She was doing her best to gnaw her bottom lip in half.

"For now." He tried to sound stern. Inside, he was chuckling. "Good day, everyone." Touching his fingers to the brim of his hat, he took his leave. "I trust I won't see any inebriated wedding guests on the road this evening."

"Absolutely not," Jake assured him.

Neil's exit was delayed by a soft, feminine hand on his arm.

Carolina's.

"Would you like a piece of cake for the road? And maybe one for your daughter? I could pull a few strings and arrange for an icing rose to be on it."

She smelled nice, the scent light and floral. He remembered it from the night they'd double-dated, when he realized his interest in her was more than casual and not at all appropriate for someone his coworker was taking out.

"Thank you, ma'am, but no." She had yet to remove her hand, and Neil could feel a slight warming where her fingers pressed into his skin.

"Okay," she said smoothly. "I guess I'll see you around, then."

Maintaining that safe distance was a lot harder when she was standing three inches away and touching him. Neil slipped up.

"I'm looking forward to it, Carolina."

"Me, too."

He returned to his car before committing a second blunder, taking her floral scent with him. The last thing he saw before pulling out of the ranch parking lot was Carolina climbing the stone walkway, the setting sun gleaming off her lime-green dress. It was a sight he wouldn't forget.

He had no sooner reached the highway when a call came in on his radio.

"Hey, Neil, you're needed back here on the double. We have a ten-twenty-four." Miss Emily was one of four dispatchers and his favorite. Perhaps because she reminded him a little of his grandmother.

"What's wrong?"

"It's a ten-thirty-five."

Miss Emily wasn't much for protocol and had been with the department too long to frazzle easily. Which was why her urgency and use of official codes concerned Neil. "Be there in twenty," he told her.

"Make it sooner."

Neil accelerated. In the eighteen months he'd been on the job, not once had he been called back to the station for an emergency, much less a confidential one. He couldn't imagine what was wrong.

The Gila County Sheriff's Station was located off the Beeline Highway, which ran through Payson. Weekend recreationists were visiting the town in record numbers, triple-digit degrees in Phoenix driving them north to the much cooler parts of the state. Growing increasingly frustrated at the constant slowdowns, Neil switched on his flashers. Traffic magically parted, and he sped the remaining distance to the station.

After parking at the rear of the building, he entered through the side door. The central room was vacant, which was almost unheard-of. Voices carried from down the hallway, loud and panicked. Neil headed in that direction. Nearly a dozen individuals were crammed in the sheriff's office, among them three other deputies, only one of whom was in uniform.

Neil scanned their worried faces. One person was noticeably missing. "Where's Sheriff Herberger?"

"That's just it." The county commissioner came out from behind the sheriff's desk to meet Neil. "He's at the Payson Regional Medical Center."

"Is he all right?"

"We hope so. He's had a heart attack."

"How bad?"

"Right now, he's stable. The doctors will know more later tonight after they run additional tests. But they say it's likely he'll require bypass surgery."

That explained the worried faces.

"What do we do?"

"The first order of business is to appoint an acting sheriff." County Commissioner Daniels placed a firm hand on Neil's shoulder. "That, my friend, is you."

"Me?"

"The City Council members and I are all in agreement. There's no one better suited to fill in for the sheriff than you."

"Excuse me, sir, but there are other deputies with more years in the department than me." Two of them were standing a few feet away and glaring at Neil.

"None with your experience in law enforcement."

"If it's all right with you—"

"Enough, Neil. We've made our decision. Congratulations." The county commissioner tightened his grip.

Neil had the uneasy sensation of being trapped.

"We've arranged for you to do an interview with KPKD," the man continued. "Tomorrow morning, nine a.m. sharp."

"So soon?"

"The people of this county need to know everything's status

quo and that they have someone competent to rely on during Sheriff Herberger's recovery."

What they had, thought Neil, was an acting sheriff who didn't want the job.

Chapter Two

Carolina arrived at work twenty minutes early, as was her habit. She liked getting a jump on the day, though lately she felt there wasn't much for her to get a jump on. While grabbing a cup of coffee in the staff lounge, she contemplated various program ideas and tried to formulate a new approach with her boss. Being shot down seven times in a row had only increased her determination to take on a greater, more respected role than that of morning traffic director.

Step one in her life-redirecting plan.

Cup in hand, she headed toward the cluster of cubicles, one of which she shared with her counterpart, the evening traffic director. A friendly voice stopped her.

"Morning, Carolina."

"Hey, Adrian."

The techie—Carolina wasn't sure of his exact title because he did a little of everything—fell in step beside her.

"How was the wedding?"

"Wonderful. Perfect. The happy couple are leaving today for a ten-day cruise of the Caribbean."

"I heard you smashed your new car."

"My niece did, actually. It's not too bad." At least that was what she kept telling herself. "I have an appointment at the body shop after work."

"Hey, listen." Adrian turned suddenly shy. "My brother

scored a couple extra tickets to the jazz concert at the casino October sixteenth. You want to go?"

Carolina flashed him a wide smile, hoping it would help ease the letdown. "Sorry, Adrian, I can't."

"Other plans?"

"Yeah." Her plans didn't involve a date but rather step two of her life-redirecting plan.

As recently as last week, she might have accepted Adrian's invitation, despite the six-year age difference. Carolina wasn't bound by convention and had dated men both younger and decades older than her.

Today, however, marked a change in policy. Henceforth, she refused to go out with anyone who didn't genuinely appeal to her—which made Neil Lovitt the only candidate.

Until yesterday she'd considered him a lost cause. But then he'd smiled at her and told her he was looking forward to seeing her again. Carolina recognized interest when she saw it. Whether Deputy Sheriff Lovitt would act on it was another thing.

Not that she was planning to wait and see. Carolina had every intention of eliciting another smile from him and finding out how far it would lead.

Her boss, the news director, poked his head around his cubicle. "Carolina. Good, you're here. I need to see you." His head promptly disappeared.

"Catch you later, Adrian."

"Sure." He lumbered off, eyes glued to the carpet, the bounce gone from his gait.

For an instant, she regretted her actions. Maybe later she'd offer to bring him back some lunch. That should help restore his good mood and reestablish that their relationship was strictly platonic.

"What's up, Ward?" She sat on the visitor chair squeezed into a narrow space between her boss's desk and the cubicle wall.

"I need you to pull double duty today. Melanie called in sick."

"Oh, okay." Carolina periodically covered for deejays. While the position was considered senior to hers, she didn't think it was anywhere near as enjoyable or challenging as the one she had in her sights—roving announcer. No being shut in a control room four hours at a stretch for her.

"We have an important interview this morning. You're going to sit in with Rowdy."

Rowdy Rodgers was the station's popular morning show host. He'd been lured away from one of Phoenix's big five in an attempt to boost KPKD's ratings and steal the number-one slot from their closest competitor.

"No problem." Carolina perked up. Coanchoring an interview with Rowdy wasn't exactly the meaty assignment she longed for, but it was a darn sight better than reading traffic reports. "Who's the guest?"

"The new acting sheriff for Gila County." Ward stared at his computer monitor while he talked, clicking his mouse and scrolling through Web pages. "We have an exclusive, so this is huge stuff."

"What happened to Sheriff Herberger?"

"He had a heart attack."

"No!"

"Yes. I want you to head over to the hospital the moment he's allowed to have visitors and interview him."

Carolina barely noticed she'd gotten her first big break. "Will he be all right?"

"That's the latest. He's having surgery today."

She made a mental note to call her cousin Jake. The family would want to send flowers.

"Who's taking his place?" she asked.

"Neil Lovitt."

"Really!"

"He's here now. They're prepping him."

Carolina suppressed the small thrill that coursed through her at the prospect of seeing Neil again so soon.

"I'll get right over there." She stood. "Thanks for the opportunity, Ward."

"Let Rowdy handle the interview. All I need from you is backup." Her boss looked up from his monitor. "Don't get carried away."

She raised two fingers in a pledge. "Scout's honor."

"Yeah, right."

His sarcastic tone wasn't lost on her, and she left his cubicle wearing a grin.

NEIL LOOKED so uncomfortable and out of place, Carolina had to bite the inside of her cheek to keep from laughing. She doubted he could sit any straighter or clench his jaw any tighter.

Without making a sound, she slid into the chair beside Rowdy. He was currently pitching a local restaurant owned by the station's newest sponsor. Without missing a beat, he pushed a sheet of paper across the table toward her. She quickly scanned the questions they would ask Neil—make that, Rowdy would ask Neil—and soundlessly set the paper down. Then she sent Neil her warmest smile.

He didn't respond. In fact, he was so focused on the microphone in front of him, he hardly acknowledged her. A line of perspiration dotted his brow, and his left hand was balled into a tight fist. Funny, she'd always thought of him as oozing confidence. It was odd seeing him so nervous.

Rowdy announced Sheriff Herberger's illness and Neil's appointment as acting sheriff, doing it all with his usual just-this-side-of-silly style.

Carolina utilized the twenty or so seconds left to study Neil and abruptly changed her mind. He wasn't nervous but rather…angry? No, uncomfortable and unhappy. And she got the feeling it wasn't because of the interview.

"Welcome to KPKD, Deputy Sheriff Lovitt. Or, should I call you *Sheriff* Lovitt now?" Rowdy opened the interview with the ease of a well-practiced professional.

"Thank you for having me."

Carolina noticed Neil didn't answer Rowdy's question.

"First off, how's Sheriff Herberger doing?" The deejay motioned for Neil to move closer and speak directly into the microphone. "I know everyone out there is concerned."

"He's doing well at the moment. His surgery is scheduled for this morning."

They went on to discuss the sheriff's prognosis. Neil's responses were clipped and to the point, demonstrating none of the skills required to make it as an on-air personality.

"Do you have any plans for the position over the next couple months?" Rowdy switched topics, a trick deejays used to keep listeners' attention.

"No."

"None at all?" Rowdy chuckled.

Neil remained stubbornly silent.

"Come on, Sheriff. This is your big chance. You could maybe wipe a few laws off the books, or how 'bout relax the dress code? Those uniforms have got to be itchy."

"I don't have that kind of authority."

"It was a joke, Sheriff."

Neil didn't so much as blink.

Rowdy shot Carolina an I'm-dying-here look.

She ignored the sheet of paper with its questions and asked one of her own. "Sheriff Lovitt, I understand you served with the NYPD for ten years. Can you tell us a little about that experience?"

His knee suddenly jerked. Coincidence, or had her question triggered the involuntary response? She decided to find out.

"I'm sure our listeners would enjoy hearing about your work in New York and how it differs from Payson. Is it anything like the show, *NYPD Blue?* And what brought you here, practically to the other side of the country?"

Another knee jerk.

She'd definitely stumbled on to something.

"The crime rate is higher in New York," he finally said.

Since Rowdy didn't seem to mind, Carolina continued with the interview. "What exactly was your position?"

"Homicide detective."

"Thank goodness we don't have much need for that here," Rowdy interjected.

"Yes."

Neil's carefully guarded control was puzzling, and Carolina liked puzzles.

"Did you ever have to shoot anybody in the line of duty?"

"Yes." The muscle in his jaw flexed.

"Often?"

"No. Just once."

Rowdy wiped imaginary sweat off his brows. "Whew! That's good to know." He signaled Carolina that he was taking back the interview.

She resigned herself to sitting quietly.

Ward's head and shoulders abruptly appeared on the other side of the glass. Because of her position, she was the only one who could see him. He pressed a sheet of notepaper to the glass. On it was written "Ask him if he's ever been shot at." When she raised her eyebrows, Ward shook his head and rolled his hand in a hurry-up gesture.

Strange, but Carolina wasn't in a position to question her boss.

"Has anyone ever shot at *you?*" she interjected during the next pause.

Neil's knee jerked again, hitting the underside of the table.

Several seconds of dead air space followed, which wasn't a good thing in radio.

Rowdy gave her an annoyed look and jumped in. "Sorry, folks. Slight technical difficulty. I think we're good now."

He pointed a finger at Carolina then placed it on his lips. She hitched a thumb at the window, mouthed *Ward* and shrugged one shoulder. Neil stared curiously at them, obviously not understanding the byplay.

"How does your daughter, Zoey, like Payson?" Rowdy read from the list of questions. "She's five, right?"

"Yes. Six next month."

"Is she in school?"

He nodded.

"The folks can't see you, Sheriff," Rowdy joked. "You have to actually talk."

"Yes, she's in school."

Ward held up another paper instructing Carolina to ask the question about being shot at again. Rowdy didn't give her a chance.

"How does she feel about her dad being appointed acting sheriff?"

"She hasn't said," Neil replied.

Ward wiggled the paper.

Carolina threw up her hands, indicating she was helpless. They'd moved on to a new topic. It made no sense going back to the old one.

All at once, Neil swung around.

Ward immediately yanked the paper down. Carolina wasn't sure if Neil had seen it or not. When he turned back around, his gaze locked with hers.

Yeah, he'd seen it all right. There was no mistaking the anger blazing in his eyes.

Rowdy conducted the rest of the interview, which lasted another two minutes, keeping it light and mildly informative—which was a credit to his talent, considering Neil didn't make it easy for the deejay.

After the interview, they went right into a song.

"Good luck, Sheriff." Rowdy shook Neil's hand. "Appreciate you dropping by today."

"No problem." Neil didn't hide his desire to get out of there as fast as possible.

Carolina tried to detain him outside the door. "I'll be interviewing Sheriff Herberger later this week. Any chance I can do a follow-up interview with you?"

"Afraid not." He inclined his head. "Have a nice day, Ms. Sweetwater."

No sexy slight curving of his lips, no murmuring her first name.

She watched him walk away, thinking she'd liked him a whole lot better yesterday.

Ward materialized from nowhere and barked in her ear, "My office, fifteen minutes!"

Good. She had a few things to discuss with him, too. Like what the heck he'd been doing waving those papers at her?

"Well?" Ward asked.

Carolina once again occupied the visitor chair in her boss's office, squished between his desk and the cubicle wall.

"It's compelling reading, but so what?" She handed him back the pages he'd printed out, copies of articles that had originally appeared in the *New York Times*.

"This is news."

"Actually, *old* news. And not necessarily relevant."

"The people of this county are entitled to know about their

new acting sheriff. The man responsible for their safety and well being."

"Know what? That his wife died tragically, the victim of a stray bullet?" Even as she said it, Carolina suffered a stab of pain. How truly awful that must have been for Neil. Not to mention his poor daughter.

"A bullet that was fired by the man he was attempting to apprehend," Ward said. "That raises some serious concerns in my mind about whether or not he acted appropriately. Whether he's the right man for the job of acting sheriff."

"According to the article, he was investigated by Internal Affairs and found innocent of any wrongdoing."

"The story is newsworthy, and it's our job to present it."

"When did KPKD get into the investigative reporting game? We're not a twenty-four-hour news station. People tune in to us to be entertained. 'Information is a perk delivered in small doses,'" she added, quoting him from a departmental meeting the previous month.

"Management wants us to raise the quality of our news segments in order to compete."

"By exploiting Neil Lovitt's personal tragedy?"

"By informing the public of a situation that concerns them."

"Surely he passed a rigorous background check when he was hired as deputy sheriff. If there had been anything ir-regular or questionable, he wouldn't have been hired."

"People lie."

Neil didn't strike Carolina as the lying type. "Why didn't you bring this up with me before the interview?"

"I just happened to do an Internet search on him."

She couldn't help gaping at Ward. "And you happened to do this *during* the interview, not before?"

"It was an afterthought. A good one."

"I still don't understand what any of this has to do with me."

While she didn't agree with Ward, he was the news director and decided what stories were read on air.

"I'm putting you in charge of the story."

"Me!"

"You have the experience."

"I'm no reporter."

"Your degree's in journalism, right?"

"Yes, but—"

"And you interned for two years at *The Arizona Republic*."

"I wrote obits and two-paragraph fillers on spelling-bee champions or Eagle Scouts. This kind of stuff is way out of my league." Not that she'd do it even if she was qualified.

"I thought you wanted more responsibility."

"I do, but not at the sake of Neil's reputation." Had it been anyone else, Carolina would have jumped at the opportunity. She liked Neil, and investigating him felt a little like betraying a friend.

"Fine." Ward rocked back in his chair. "Then I'll give someone else the Sheriff Herberger interview."

Her mouth fell open. "That's blackmail."

"That's reassigning. And my prerogative as news director."

"Why me?" Her indignation was turning into anger. She didn't like being manipulated.

"Because Neil Lovitt likes you."

"Hardly."

"He does, and he's more likely to let his guard down with someone he likes."

Manipulating her *and* Neil. "What if we—"

He cut her short with a raised hand. "I've made my decision. It's your story. End of discussion."

She refrained from saying more. For the moment.

"Get moving," he told her. "You're on again in four minutes."

Carolina went to her own cubicle around the corner and familiarized herself with the latest traffic update. Her heart, however, wasn't in it. As expected, there were no changes from earlier. Traffic was slow and go in the center of town, and an RV with engine trouble was creating delays on the highway just outside of town.

Glancing at her watch, she noted the time and jumped from her chair, shoving it just a little too hard. The loud screech caused two heads to pop up over the cubicle walls.

"Sorry."

She hurried down the hall, waging a silent war with herself. Ward didn't make idle threats. If she refused this assignment, he might fire her, claiming insubordination. He'd done it before.

How could he not see there was nothing more than a sad, heart-wrenching story in the death of Neil's wife? Then again, Neil *had* responded oddly several times during the interview and didn't appear happy about his temporary promotion.

Could there really be more going on with him than immediately apparent?

Her old journalistic itch unwillingly returned.

Damn Ward. He was probably counting on that.

NEIL'S FIRST DAY as acting sheriff wasn't going well, not that he'd expected anything different after the interview with Rowdy and Carolina. Fortunately, his shift was almost over.

Lifting the phone to his ear, he pushed a button on the dial pad. A generic female voice told him, "You have forty-six new messages. Press number sign to—"

He disconnected before the voice could finish.

When he'd first arrived at the station after leaving KPKD, he'd listened to the two dozen messages already waiting for him and taken another dozen calls before issuing instructions that all nonemergencies be sent directly to his voice mail. The congratulations were nice, if tedious. Even the complaints and angry rants didn't bother him.

It was the threat to resign or else that got to him, turning his blood to ice and releasing a flood of unwelcome memories.

Neil had no idea if the anonymous caller was serious—the threat wasn't specific, only saying he'd regret accepting the position of acting sheriff, but he'd refused to take any chances and immediately reported the incident.

He pushed another button on his phone. "Mary, can you come in here, please."

"Yes, sir."

Mary Twohorses, Sheriff Herberger's—and now Neil's— secretary, padded into his office, amazingly light on her feet for a woman of such generous proportions. She'd started with the sheriff's department back when two small rooms served as headquarters and typewriters were used in place of computers. "Can I help you with something?"

"Go through my voice messages from today, please. Delete the unimportant ones and make note of the calls I need to return."

"Of course."

"There are a lot of them."

"No problem."

She wore the same patient smile she always did. Nothing ruffled Mary Twohorses's feathers, for which Neil was glad. It had taken him less than an hour on the job this morning to realize he'd be lost without her.

"Thank you." He opened the top right drawer and retrieved his few personal possessions.

"Are you leaving for the day?" she asked.

"Yeah. I have to pick up my daughter from after-school

day care." He pocketed his cell phone and keys. "Is R.J. here yet?"

"Just arrived."

"Good."

Mary followed Neil down the hall as far as her office. She would normally have gone home already but was staying late to help with the transition. In the central room, Neil met up with R.J., his lead deputy and the one in charge tonight, and quickly briefed him before leaving by way of the rear door.

The ride to the elementary school his daughter attended didn't take long. He swung into the main parking lot and joined the long line of vehicles already there. A few minutes later, Zoey, along with a crowd of about twenty-five children, burst through the double glass doors. They were closely monitored by a trio of energetic day-care workers. Zoey was released only when Neil stepped out of the patrol car and came around to the passenger side.

She skipped over to him, clutching a packet of papers as if they were constructed of spun gold while dragging her Hello Kitty backpack on the ground. The hair her babysitter, Carmen, had so carefully arranged that morning hung down into her face. Her T-shirt was rumpled and stained with what Neil guessed was finger paint, and her sneaker laces were untied.

He ignored her disarray. To him, his daughter looked adorable.

"Daddy, Daddy!" She delicately peeled the papers away from her chest and waved them at Neil. "Look."

"How about a hug first?" He bent down to her level.

She obliged his request. When he would have held her a moment longer, she pulled away. "You have to read this."

As if he could. The papers were upside down and moving from side to side. He did manage to recognize the Kinder Kids logo, the after-school activity club to which Zoey belonged.

He assumed the papers were information about another field trip to the movies or the museum.

"Okay. When we get home."

"No, now. Pretty please," she added, her small china-doll face filled with excitement and anticipation. "It's really important."

"I have to drive." Her profound disappointment tugged at him while he buckled her into the passenger seat, walked around the car and climbed in behind the steering wheel. "Why don't you tell me what it says," he suggested and turned the key.

Her blue eyes, so much like her mother's, lit up. "They're giving riding lessons. Every Saturday. Can I go?"

"I need to know more before I say yes." Cost wasn't the issue. Neither was transporting Zoey, though it could be complicated while his schedule remained up in the air.

His daughter's safety was his biggest concern. The anonymous caller hadn't mentioned Zoey but until Neil found out if the threat he'd received today was real or a prank, he wasn't about to let her go anywhere except to school without him.

"You promised," Zoey complained. "You said when we moved here I could learn to ride a horse."

She was right. He had, in fact, made several promises in an effort to ease their relocation from New York to Arizona. Ones he'd since come to reconsider. She'd begged him for a pony. He had appeased her with an offer of riding lessons. But that was before he saw how big horses were and how tiny and vulnerable his daughter looked sitting on top of them.

"I've taken you riding. Twice." He joined the line of exiting vehicles loaded with their cargos of children.

"A pony ride at the fair doesn't count."

"What about that time at Carmen's cousin's house? You had fun."

"Which is why I want to go again."

She sounded too adult to be just five-going-on-six. Old enough, he supposed, to take riding lessons. The after-school program wouldn't be offering them to students unless there was minimal risk, right?

Why didn't she want a kitten or to be a ballerina like other little girls?

"I'll go over the paperwork when we get home. See how much the lessons cost, what time they are and how long they last." If they were only an hour, he would stay and watch Zoey. *Closely.* "Wintergreen Stables isn't too far from home."

"That's not where they're having them." Zoey studied the papers, her brow furrowed and her mouth pursed. Despite her efforts, Neil doubted she could read more than a couple dozen words. "Miss Meyers said Bear Creek Ranch."

"Huh. Really?"

Well, that threw a whole new light on the subject. After the interview this morning, Neil wasn't sure he wanted to cross paths with Carolina again. Not until Sheriff Herberger returned to work. She'd asked too many personal questions. Questions Neil hadn't wanted to answer.

On the other hand, what were the chances she'd be at the ranch when he was there with Zoey? Probably nil. Certainly not enough for him to break a promise he'd made to his daughter.

"I'm not saying yes, mind you," Neil told Zoey. "But if everything works out, you can take lessons. For a while, anyway. Then we'll see how it goes."

"Thank you, Daddy." She leaned across the seat as far as her seat belt would allow and hugged his arm. "I love you."

"Love you, too, kiddo."

Neil hoped he didn't regret his decision. Carolina's probing questions weren't his main reason for avoiding her.

It was the temptation she presented and what could happen if he gave in to it.

The threatening call had served to remind him of the dangers associated with his job and his commitment to keep the people he cared about safe. Something he'd failed to do with his late wife.

Protecting Zoey might prove difficult, but protecting Carolina was another story. He just had to stay the hell away from her.

Chapter Three

Carolina stood at the foot of Sheriff Herberger's hospital bed and listened to him answer Rowdy's questions. An earbud attached to a tiny portable transmitter allowed her to hear both ends of the interview, though the echo effect was disorienting.

A firm grip on the bed rail and a tapping right foot allowed her to vent a little of the frustration building inside her.

Ward hadn't been completely forthright with her the other day, which made his strong-arming her into doing an investigative piece on Neil all the more unconscionable. Carolina wasn't interviewing Sheriff Herberger as much as babysitting him, a task one of the techies like Adrian could have easily handled. The questions she'd been given for the sheriff were actually being asked by Rowdy. Her job was limited to going over the list with Sheriff Herberger before the interview and coaching him with his responses if necessary.

Right. The sheriff might have undergone major surgery two days ago, but twenty-six years as an elected official had honed his public-speaking skills, enabling him to carry off a simple radio interview with ease.

Carolina watched him and wavered between telling Ward off when she got back to the station or being a good girl and just shutting up. This could be a test, she reasoned. If she pitched a fit, Ward could use her reaction to shoot down her next bid for a better assignment…and the next, and the next.

If they turned out like the one she was doing on Neil, maybe she should consider changing careers.

A few tentative forays into researching the death of his wife had produced little more than what Ward had already learned and nothing that implicated Neil. Carolina hoped additional digging would provide the same. Then she'd go to Ward and tell him she couldn't find dirt because there wasn't any.

She tried not to think about the—in her opinion, nonexistent—possibility that Neil had acted irresponsibly and caused his wife's death.

Sheriff Herberger caught her eye. She smiled encouragingly, giving him a silent thumbs-up. For someone who'd just had a heart attack followed by a triple bypass, he looked good.

Then again, the man was made of granite, as his record proved. He'd seen a lot of change in the past quarter century and endured his share of difficulties, both professional and personal. He'd stood strong for what he believed in, even when those beliefs weren't popular, and was a staunch advocate for the rights of the people who'd elected him.

He was also a longtime friend of the Tuckers, especially Carolina's uncle, who'd managed the ranch before her cousin Jake took over. From tales her uncle told, he and the sheriff had run around together as teenagers and young Otis Herberger had tangled once or twice with the law before deciding to switch sides.

"Well, thanks for having me today, Rowdy," he said into the phone.

"We're glad to hear you're doing well."

While the sheriff and Rowdy were wrapping up the interview, Carolina's thoughts drifted to the station and what she'd say to Ward when she got back. It took a moment for her brain to register that Neil's name had been mentioned.

"I'd be back on the job tomorrow if those dang doctors would let me," Sheriff Herberger continued. "In the meantime, I'm sure Deputy Sheriff Lovitt will do a bang-up job, no pun intended."

The sheriff and Rowdy both laughed.

"He's kind of a serious guy, isn't he?" Rowdy asked.

"When it comes to work, yes. But off duty, he can relax and kick back with the best of them." Sheriff Herberger glanced at Carolina and winked.

She felt her cheeks warm. Did he know about the double date she and Neil had shared last year? Touching a finger to her earbud, she smiled back while trying to appear preoccupied with the broadcast.

The sheriff and Rowdy exchanged a few final comments, then said goodbye. Carolina went over to the sheriff and helped him hang up the phone, which was on the nightstand and beyond his reach.

"How'd I do?"

"You were great." She patted his arm, the one without tubes and monitors attached to it. "A real pro."

"I hate this." His smile dissolved. "I've never been sick a day in my life. And now…" He laid his head back on the pillow and closed his eyes. In that moment, he looked his age and then some. "Three months' mandatory leave of absence. I don't know if I'll be able to hold up without going crazy."

The door cracked open, and a nurse peeked in. Carolina waved to her, and she entered, brandishing yet another floral arrangement. "I didn't want to interrupt if you were still doing the interview." She went over to the dresser.

"No problem, we're done."

The nurse moved two arrangements to make room for the new one.

"It's starting to look like a damn funeral parlor in here," the sheriff grumbled.

"You should be glad it's not a funeral parlor," Carolina said.

"You're right." He laughed again. "Be sure to tell your family thank you for the flowers they sent."

"I will."

The nurse left. Carolina would give anything to do the same, but figured she might not have another opportunity to be alone with the sheriff for a long time. Besides, if Ward asked, she could tell him with complete honesty she was working on the story about Neil.

"We did a little research on Deputy Sheriff Lovitt before his interview the other day."

"Is that so?"

"To help us with questions." She winced at the bald-faced lie. Fortunately, the sheriff didn't appear to notice. "I read about his wife's death."

Sheriff Herberger shook his head sympathetically. "A truly terrible accident."

"I saw that he was investigated by Internal Affairs."

"Standard procedure. Nothing more. Neil acted properly and in the line of duty. There were also more than twenty civilians who witnessed the incident."

"Is it normal for an off-duty police officer to go after a suspect?" Carolina hated to admit it but she was becoming curious, from a strictly personal standpoint. "Especially out in the open like that with lots of people in the area?"

"Protecting the public doesn't stop just because a law enforcement officer clocks out. He had a responsibility."

"I suppose you're right."

"Neil's a good cop." The sheriff yawned. "He'll be a great acting sheriff."

"Of course." She gathered the rest of her things. "You're tired. I'll leave and let you rest."

His thick salt-and-pepper eyebrows came together in a pronounced V. "Is there some reason for your curiosity about Neil?"

"I'd like to know that, too."

Carolina whirled at the familiar voice. The slight embarrassment she'd felt earlier with Sheriff Herberger was nothing compared to now.

Neil stood in the doorway. On second thought, *filled* the doorway was a better description. There were two inches of empty space between his shoulders and the doorjamb. She involuntarily swallowed.

"Neil!" Sheriff Herberger instantly perked up. "Did you hear the interview?"

"No, sorry. I was in the E.R."

"Someone hurt?" The sheriff became instantly alert, all signs of drowsiness gone.

"A hiker took a fall near Windy Canyon. Nothing serious but we brought him in just to be on the safe side." He shot Carolina a piercing look.

She straightened her spine, not about to let him see his unexpected arrival had unnerved her. "Good morning, Sheriff Lovitt. Sheriff Herberger and I were just chatting about you."

"So I heard." He didn't move except for his eyes, which tracked her as she slid away from the head of the bed. "If you have any questions about me, I'd rather you ask me directly and not trouble other people."

"Good idea." Sheriff Herberger's weary face broke into a grin, and he shooed them out of the room. "It's about lunchtime. I hear the cafeteria makes a decent cheeseburger, not that my doctor will let me have one."

"I really need to get back to the station." Carolina made the excuse, thinking she was saving Neil an awkward situation.

He took her completely aback when he said, "Lunch sounds great," and stepped aside to let her pass. "My treat."

THE CAFETERIA WAS CROWDED and noisy. Not exactly the best place for a personal discussion. But, then, was there ever a good place to lay open old wounds?

One good thing, Neil thought as he bit into his club sandwich, the food was decent. He'd wolfed down most of it, which meant he couldn't put off talking with Carolina much longer.

He still wasn't sure how much he'd tell her. Generally, he didn't care what other people thought of him. The months of living beneath a microscope after Lynne's death had thickened his skin. But of everyone he'd met in Payson, Carolina was the one person besides Sheriff Herberger that he wanted to know the truth and not some distorted version of it. Why her opinion of him counted, he wasn't sure, but it did.

She ate her tuna salad, patiently waiting for him to start. He liked that about her. He'd found most people in the media to be pushy and high energy. Carolina had an appealing calm about her, though he sensed she wasn't a softie by any means.

Amazing that some lucky guy hadn't swept her off her feet and slipped a ring on her finger. She must have had her share of offers.

Neil polished off the last of his sandwich with some milk.

"You going to eat all of those?" Carolina asked, eyeing his French fries.

"Help yourself."

She did—to three large ones, dunking them in the leftover pool of ketchup on his plate before popping them into her mouth. It was something his daughter, Zoey, would do.

He chuckled.

"What?"

"You."

"I gave up fries a while back. Too many carbs." Carolina smiled coyly. "Sometimes my willpower gives out."

He started to answer, then stopped, realizing she'd asked for the fries more to put him at ease than to satisfy any food craving. It was enough to break the ice.

"His name was John Leity," Neil began without preamble. "A normal-sounding name, a normal-looking guy. If you were standing behind him in line at the grocery store, you wouldn't think him guilty of anything more serious than an unpaid parking ticket. We called him the Delivery Man because that was his method of entry. No one was afraid of his face when they saw it through a peephole."

"He was a serial killer."

"Suspected of raping and killing seven women, slitting their throats and leaving them to bleed out on their apartment floors."

Carolina gasped softly and placed her folded hands in her lap.

"There was also sufficient DNA evidence to tie him to a string of other, lesser crimes." Neil absently rubbed his thumb up and down his glass of milk, removing the condensation. "We'd been searching for him for six months. He always managed to remain one step ahead of us."

Neil paused. It had been years since he'd told anyone the entire story. Emotions long buried rushed to the surface, and he needed a moment to rein them in.

"Lynne and I were having a late brunch at a neighborhood outdoor deli. They had the best lox and bagel in the city, and she liked to go there on my days off." The memory struck a gentle chord in his heart. "Zoey was asleep in her stroller, which was parked beside our table. Lynne and I were talking,

I don't even remember about what, when I suddenly looked up and saw the Delivery Man at the newsstand across the street." He involuntarily tensed, much like he had that day. "I didn't believe it at first. His regular territory was forty blocks away."

"What did you do?"

He'd gone after the guy. Carolina knew that. He decided to tell her what she didn't know, what very few people outside the NYPD did.

"I told Lynne what was going on and pulled out my cell phone. I wanted to call in his location before he got too far away. She grabbed the phone and told me to go after him."

"That was very brave of her."

"It was." The background din of the busy cafeteria faded into nothingness as Neil relived that horrific day. "You'd have thought with all the violent crimes she dealt with in her own work, she'd have been afraid. For Zoey, if not for herself. But Lynne understood the importance of catching that bastard before he killed another girl."

"What did she do for a living?"

"She was a crime scene investigations analyst. She took an extended leave of absence when she was pregnant. I wish now she'd gone back to work. We might not have been at the deli that day."

"I don't remember reading anywhere she was a cop."

"The media somehow always forgot to mention it. Painting me as the irresponsible cop husband willing to endanger his wife and child sold newspapers and raised TV ratings." Anger and bitterness roughened his voice, and he cleared his throat. "It was bad enough I lost Lynne. Worse that I played a direct part in her death and would have to live with the guilt and grief. But the media went out of its way to make my life a living hell."

"I'm so sorry."

A lot of people had spoken those words to him. Few with as much sincerity.

"A group of *concerned citizens* thought I should be fired for being remiss in my duty. The really screwy thing is, according to protocol, I would have been remiss in my duty if I hadn't gone after the guy."

Neil forced himself to relax and breathe deeply. The air in the cafeteria had become stifling. When he could talk again, he said, "I was almost on him when he spotted me. I figured he'd run, especially when I pulled my gun. Hell, who wouldn't run?"

"But he didn't?"

"Turned and hit me like a three-hundred-pound defensive tackle. People scattered like a bomb had exploded. I went down hard on the concrete but got a hold of his pant leg. He shook me loose and cut back across the street instead of disappearing into the crowd."

"Toward the deli?"

He could hear the horror in Carolina's voice. It wasn't unlike the horror gripping his chest, freezing his heart. The kind he experienced every time he recalled what happened next.

"I ran after him. He fired two shots at me. I…didn't realize he had a gun—he'd always used a knife on the girls—though I'm not sure it would have made a difference. I was operating on pure adrenaline by then. The second bullet grazed my scalp. I returned fire. And didn't miss." Neil concentrated on the condiments clustered in the middle of their table, sensing Carolina's gaze on him, feeling her compassion. "The same bullet that winged me hit the building and ricocheted off… into Lynne's neck. A quarter inch to the left, and it would have missed the artery. She was dead before the ambulance arrived. Loss of blood. Like all his victims."

"Oh, Neil." Carolina laid a warm hand over his.

He didn't flinch or withdraw, his usual reaction. Instead, he absorbed the sympathy she offered, letting it fill some of the hollow places inside him.

"I was suspended until the investigation was complete, basically for my protection. And Zoey's. After I was cleared to return to work, the department was flooded with letters and phone calls, demanding I be fired. I saved them the trouble and resigned ten months later."

"What did you do after that?"

"Went and got Zoey from her grandparents. I was a mess when Lynne died. Physically and emotionally. I thought I couldn't take care of Zoey and that she'd be safer away from me and the city. Lynne's parents live in upstate New York and adore Zoey. They were happy to have her."

"Giving her up must have been really hard for you."

"It was. I managed because it was temporary." He paused a moment before making his most important point. "I don't want Zoey growing up hearing the details of her mother's death and my part in it. I'll do whatever's necessary to prevent it." He ground out the last sentence.

"She doesn't know how Lynne died?"

"Only that it was an accidental shooting."

"It's not my place to ask, but do you think that's wise?"

"She's too young to understand."

"She won't always be young."

"I won't have Zoey hate me because she blames me for her mother's death."

"You weren't the one who fired the gun that killed Lynne. The Delivery Man did."

"Because I went after him."

"Zoey loves you. She won't hold you responsible."

"Maybe. Maybe not. I'm not taking any chances."

"She may find out on her own one day. It won't be hard. You're all over the Internet. Are you ready for that?"

Carolina had just voiced Neil's biggest fear. "You're right about what you said earlier. It's not your place to ask."

"I apologize."

"Zoey is everything to me. More important than my career. She's the reason I quit the force, took a year off and rented an apartment in the same town as my in-laws so that Zoey and I could be close to them. When I stopped seeing Lynne's blood covering the sidewalk every night in my dreams, I figured I was ready to go back to work. It took me another six months to find the job I was looking for."

"Deputy sheriff?" Carolina removed her hand from his.

Neil wished she hadn't. Her fingers had felt nice resting on his. "For a while I considered getting out of law enforcement altogether or going into a related field, like security. Then I'd remember Lynne and her commitment. She believed with all her heart we were making the world a better place. Me by catching criminals and her by processing the evidence that helped put them behind bars. I decided to stay in law enforcement to honor her."

"She would be proud of you."

"I couldn't stay in the city. Zoey's safety is my main concern." He thought of the threatening phone call from the other day. Fortunately, there had been no more. "Rural law enforcement seemed like a good fit. Gila County has its share of trouble, but not like New York. I swore I would never put myself or my family in jeopardy again."

"Is that why you don't want to be acting Sheriff?"

Leave it to Carolina to figure him out.

"One thing I've learned, the higher profile the position, the greater the danger. There are too many wackos out there, and they tend to target those in charge."

"I see now why you didn't like being interviewed."

"My relationship with the media isn't a good one."

"After what you've been through, no one could expect

differently." She glanced away, then back at him. "I suppose I should explain myself."

"Not if you don't want to."

"I owe you that much after everything you've told me." She sighed. "You won't like it. I sure don't."

"Try me."

"I've been assigned to do a story on you."

"I see," he said flatly.

"My boss inferred that if I don't do the story, my job could be on the line."

Even though he'd already decided not to pursue a relationship with Carolina, he'd stupidly hoped her interest in him was personal. Well, this definitely clinched it. Steering clear of her would be much simpler from now on. If he weren't sitting down, he'd give himself a swift kick in the rear. He pushed back his chair, well aware he was about to be rude but not caring. "I guess I've just given you everything you need for your story." He was surprised at how much it angered him that Carolina was the one about to bring his world crashing down around him.

"No, Neil." She reached over the small table for his arm, gripping it tightly. "You've just given me every reason to tell my boss exactly where he can shove this assignment."

"You'd give up your job for me?"

"I have my integrity."

Her eyes shone with sincerity and her voice rang with conviction.

So why did Neil feel he still couldn't trust her?

Chapter Four

"Are you crazy!" Rachel looked stunned.

"I don't usually agree with Rachel," Vi said, "but seriously, kiddo, have you thought this through?"

"It so happens I have."

Carolina took her older sisters' criticism in stride. She'd expected nothing less than shock and outrage from her family when she'd informed them of the run-in with her boss after lunch with Neil. The only one of them who might have understood her reasons was Corrine. She, however, was still cruising the Caribbean with her new husband and wouldn't be back for several more days.

"What if you lose your job?" Vi asked.

She was the oldest of the four sisters and the first to make their mother's fondest wish come true by giving her a grandchild. A girl. No surprise there, the Tucker-Sweetwater clan was overrun with members of the fairer sex. Even their cousin Jake, the lone male in their generation, had produced four daughters. With Carolina and Rachel still single and Vi having trouble getting pregnant a second time, all hopes were now pinned on Corrine to break the trend.

"I won't lose my job." Carolina tried to convey a confidence she was far from feeling. Ward had made his displeasure at her defiance abundantly clear. She was still smarting from his verbal reprimand. "If he was going to fire me, he'd have done it already."

"Maybe not. He could be waiting." Jake stepped out onto the redwood deck, carrying a plastic pitcher of fruit punch and a bag of potato chips. He'd invited his cousins over for a lazy Saturday afternoon of hanging out in his backyard and enjoying the spectacular mountain views. The girls had insisted on playing in the hot tub. Briana was recruited to supervise them in exchange for getting a day shaved off her punishment. She'd been grounded a month for the parking lot fender bender.

"Waiting for what?" Carolina sipped her iced tea. She'd contemplated asking for a beer but was afraid it might look as if she was drowning her sorrows.

"You to quit," Jake said.

"Why would I quit?"

Jake set the fruit punch and chips down on a picnic table beside the hot tub. His three oldest daughters, along with Vi's rambunctious preschooler, scrambled from the hot tub in a noisy, chaotic frenzy. Leaving a trail of puddles and wet footprints in their wake, they pounced on the snack as if they hadn't eaten in days. The only one missing was Jake's youngest. A year old, she was much too little to swim in the hot tub with her sisters and cousin. She and her mother had gone into town for some shopping, leaving Jake in charge of keeping the masses entertained.

"Here. Put these on before you catch cold." Vi jumped up from her chaise longue and handed the girls towels, making sure to wrap up her daughter snugly.

"This isn't Denver, Vi," Rachel admonished. "It's, what, seventy-two?"

Jake tipped his chair back and studied the thermometer mounted beside the door. "More like seventy-eight."

"How quickly they forget." Rachel laughed. "Fall in Arizona is like summer everywhere else."

Carolina's relief that the subject had veered from her current work dilemma didn't last. Jake refused to let it go.

"Your boss might try and force you to quit," he said, shooting her a quelling look, "by making your job a living hell."

"Don't swear in front of the girls," Vi hissed.

"Sorry."

"I doubt Ward would pressure me like that. It would be considered harassment, and the station has a no-harassment policy." Carolina leaned forward and reached for a chip, promising herself she'd have just one. A half dozen magically jumped into her open hand.

"Not necessarily," Jake answered. "Depends on how he went about it."

"What would be the benefit of me quitting versus firing me?"

"He wouldn't have to give you severance pay, for starters. And you probably couldn't collect unemployment."

"Humph. I'm not sure even Ward's that devious. He's more of an explode one minute and forget about it the next kind of manager." More potato chips appeared in Carolina's hand and made their way to her mouth. "That's why I think if he hasn't fired me by now, he won't. Of course, I can forget about any more special assignments or promotions." The last chip lodged in her throat as that dismal reality sank in, and she coughed to clear it.

"I think you should quit," Vi said hotly. "You have way too much talent for that dinky station."

Big sisters. Hate them one minute, love them the next.

"What would I do for a job? The other stations in town aren't hiring or I'd have heard."

"We're shorthanded in the office."

Jake's suggestion earned him a disgruntled groan. "Work

for you? No, thank you. Helping Mom is enough." Like most of the family members, Carolina split herself between the ranch and an outside job. In her case, she assisted her mother, Millie, who was in charge of their many and frequently elaborate weddings. "Besides, I like working at the station. Most of the time," she added. "I'm not ready to throw in the towel yet."

"Just in case, I think you should give Howard a call," Jake said.

Carolina frowned at the mention of the family's attorney.

"What all did this new acting sheriff say that would make you go against your boss?" Vi asked.

Carolina reminded herself that her sister had moved away from Bear Creek Ranch almost ten years ago, and although she returned regularly to visit, she hadn't met Neil yet.

"You wouldn't ask that question if you saw him." Rachel's radiant grin spoke volumes.

"Oh."

"Yeah," Carolina concurred with a sigh.

"What?" Jake looked from one to the other, his expression befuddled. "Is this some sort of female code?"

"Neil Lovitt is hot," Rachel translated for him.

"Seriously hot," Briana chimed in, plopping down on the end of Carolina's chaise longue. Her younger sisters, evidently reenergized from their snack, had returned to the hot tub, their little cousin in tow. "For, you know, an older guy and everything."

"Old?" Jake recoiled. "What does that make me?"

Briana rolled her eyes and turned her attention back to Carolina. "I don't blame you for refusing to do the story. He's really nice and doesn't deserve to have his reputation trashed."

"He is nice." Carolina smiled. "And not just because he cut you some slack with that ticket." The things Neil had told her about his late wife's death and raising his daughter alone had deeply affected her. She hadn't been able to stop thinking about him since their conversation.

"Is that your only reason?" Jake asked.

"Absolutely." Carolina instantly put up her guard. She and Jake weren't merely related, they were good friends. He knew her as well as, if not better than, her sisters. "He's a nice guy, as Briana says, with a sad past. What other reason do I need?"

"You forgot to mention hot." Rachel, still grinning, rubbed sunscreen onto her bare arms.

Jake's gaze narrowed on Carolina. "I know for a fact there are a lot of nice, *hot* people with sad pasts that you wouldn't risk your job for."

She didn't answer him—which was a mistake because it became immediately obvious that everybody present over the age of ten suspected there was more to her motives for defending Neil than she'd admitted. Close families definitely had their drawbacks.

"Be careful," Jake warned. "No reason to screw up your life for some guy you hardly know."

"Language, please." Vi glowered at Jake. Again.

Carolina pondered Jake's point while he and her sister debated whether or not Vi's daughter had already heard the words he'd used at preschool.

Neil wasn't "some guy" as far as Carolina was concerned. She definitely experienced a connection with him, of the zing-clear-to-her-toes caliber. The connection could, she feared, be one-sided. He hadn't exactly bubbled over with joy in the hospital cafeteria when she'd promised him she would defy her boss and not do the story on him. If anything, he'd appeared hesitant to believe her and had required considerable convincing on her part.

Carolina liked to think of herself as a good-hearted person, but Jake was right. She wouldn't lay her job on the line for just anyone. It prompted her to wonder exactly how strong her attraction to Neil was and what, if anything, she should do about it.

"Let me see how Ward acts on Monday," she said, speaking over Jake and Vi's silly argument. "He might not mention the story again. Depending on how it goes, I may call Howard."

"Good." Her declaration appeared to satisfy Jake. "I'll be right back," he said when the trill of a phone sounded through the partially open door. "Briana, watch the girls, please."

Rachel waited until Jake was inside to pin Carolina down. "So, you going to ask him out?"

"No!"

"Why not? You want to go out with him."

"She may *want* to go out with him—" Vi sent her sister a superior look reminiscent of when they were teens "—but that doesn't mean she prefers to do the asking."

Briana, who hadn't returned to the hot tub, vacillated between watching the younger girls and observing the adult goings-on with starstruck fascination.

"You know me." Carolina lifted one shoulder in a casual shrug. "If a man appeals to me, I have no qualms about making the first move."

"That's true," Vi agreed, "if you don't like him all that much. If you do, then you suddenly go from laughing in the face of convention to strictly traditional."

Carolina winced. "I do not."

"Come on, sis. When's the last time you hesitated about taking the initiative?"

She could pinpoint the day exactly. It had been on her disastrous double date with Neil. She'd hoped he would pick up on her attraction to him and respond in kind. Luckily, she hadn't shared the details of that night with her sisters. Or not luckily, she thought, after hearing Vi's next remark.

"It was Lonnie, right?"

Not that Carolina was having fun in the first place, but why did her sister have to bring up the dreaded ex-fiancé?

"I'm sure there's been someone else I've hesitated to ask out since him." There *had* to be. Carolina racked her brain and came up blank. Uh-oh. Her sisters were right. She really did like Neil. Damn!

"I think one of the girls got water up her nose," she said, but her plan for distracting the four unwavering stares fixed on her failed. "I can't concentrate with all this pressure."

"See?" Vi sat back in her chair. "Told you."

"Aunt Carolina's crushing," Briana said in a singsong tone.

"I'm not crushing on Neil." Carolina was afraid it might be far worse. Like total and complete infatuation.

"So, prove us wrong and ask him out."

Jake's timing couldn't have been better. She'd never felt so glad to see him come through a door.

"Hey, you're—" she began to say, but the disturbed look on his face stopped her midsentence. "What's wrong?"

"That was Gary on the phone," Jake said, referring to their manager of guest amenities. He started picking up damp towels and hanging them on the railing to dry. "Come on, girls, we have to go inside. Party's over."

"Aw, Dad," his daughters chorused.

"Sorry. Something important came up."

Sensing his urgency, Carolina rose and began to help. "What did he say?"

Gary had been an employee for over thirty years and knew the operation of the ranch better than anyone except the immediate family. For him to phone Jake at home signaled a serious problem.

"Little José was on the north ridge this morning where it butts up against federal land checking the high trails before the weather turns." Clearing trails of debris was a task the ranch hands regularly performed every March and October. "He found something. Gary drove out there this afternoon to verify it in case Little José was wrong. He wasn't."

"Jeez, Jake." Rachel jumped up and also started helping. "You talk like he discovered a dead body."

"No, not that."

"Thank goodness."

"It was evidence of illegal mining."

"LOOK FOR A NUMBERED marker around the next bend."

"Gotcha."

Neil downshifted into a lower gear and floored the gas. The Jeep bounced and banged over rocks and rain washes with every foot of rugged mountain terrain they covered. Veering sharply to the right, he narrowly avoided a sprawling ponderosa. As it was, a low-hanging branch scraped across the Jeep's canvas top. The noise was momentarily deafening.

"Take it easy, will you?" Neil's deputy, R.J., flopped around in the front passenger seat. Clutching the grab bar, he jammed the soles of both feet into the floorboard. "I'd like to get there with all my bones intact, if you don't mind."

Neil shifted again as they crested the top of a small hill. The trail they'd taken was minimally maintained, narrow and designed for horses or ATVs, not full-size vehicles. The fact he and R.J. had made it this far was a testament to the Jeep's sturdiness and, Neil liked to think, his ability as a driver.

He'd discovered a passion for off-road driving soon after moving to Payson, never having encountered anything like it in New York City or the outskirts of Schenectady, where he'd grown up. The sheriff's department's standard issue Jeep didn't compare to his own tricked-out, four-wheel-drive pickup, but he still pushed the older vehicle for everything it had, relishing the rush of adrenaline surging through him.

Challenging himself with an almost unnavigable trail had the added benefit of keeping troublesome thoughts at bay—like Carolina and her promise not to do the story on him. He still didn't know whether he could believe her or not. And her warning that his daughter would learn the part he'd played in her mother's death was disrupting his sleep, dulling his appetite and affecting his mood. He'd have to be more careful in the future. Just this morning at breakfast Zoey had asked him if anything was wrong. He hated lying to her, but what choice did he have?

"Are you on a suicide mission or what?" R.J. swore as the GPS device he'd been holding went flying.

"This is nothing," Neil answered. And it was.

"Says you."

"Hang on!" He cranked the steering wheel hard to the left.

Thankfully, the old Jeep didn't let him down. Its tires hugged the ground, sending dirt and small rocks spraying in every direction. The sense of power revived Neil, and he wished he could control everything in his life with the same ease he did the Jeep.

"Damn it to hell," R.J. complained when his cowboy hat collided with the sun visor, shoving the brim down over his eyes. He pushed it back up and blinked. "Slow down, for Pete's sake. We're not in a race."

Neil let up on the gas only when they reached the top of the next small hill. At the bottom a pair of pickup trucks and three ATVs were parked, reminding him that the reason for their wilderness adventure was business, not pleasure.

He pulled up alongside the closest truck and cut the engine. Two men—one young, one older, neither of whom he recognized—were removing kerosene lanterns from a crate in the bed of the truck and lighting them. Good thing. The sun was quickly disappearing beneath the distant mountaintops, and any minute now they would be swallowed by darkness and surrounded by cold.

Across the gully, seven more people had gathered together on a slope that looked no different than the half-dozen others in the immediate area—except for the crude, gaping hole in the side, four feet high by three feet wide. Neil was no authority, but even he realized the hole was not a product of Mother Nature.

He and R.J. exited the Jeep. Opening the rear compartment, they grabbed their jackets, a pair of flashlights, a toolbox and a roll of yellow crime-scene tape before parting ways. Neil joined the two men lighting lanterns while R.J. battled trees and a dense thicket to reach the group of people standing in front of the hole. Most of them had their backs to Neil. Even so, he recognized Jake Tucker's unmistakable stance.

"Evening." Neil addressed the men beside the truck.

The older of the two glanced at the badge on Neil's shirt and extended his hand. "Howdy, Sheriff. I'm Gary Forester, and this is Little José. He's the fellow who found the shaft."

Neil reached inside his jacket and removed a notebook. "Can you tell me more about that?"

"I was riding the trail, looking for areas that needed clearing."

"Where's your horse now?" Neil scribbled as Little José talked.

"We trailered him back to the ranch so I didn't have to ride in the dark."

"How did you happen to notice the mine shaft?" Out of the corner of his eye, Neil observed R.J. attempting to remove the people from the slope and the crime scene. He was being met with some resistance, from Jake in particular.

"I *didn't* notice it," Little José said. "Not at first. What I found was this." He lifted one of the lanterns, illuminating the truck's lowered tailgate where a long, cylindrical piece of iron lay. "It was right there in the middle of the trail."

Neil fished a handkerchief from his back pocket. "Who else besides you has touched this?" he asked.

"Just Gary."

Careful not to smudge any possible fingerprints and incur the wrath of the CSI team, Neil used the handkerchief to lift the object. His hand dipped slightly at the unexpected weight.

"It's a chisel," Little José informed him.

"And finding this prompted you to go looking for a mine shaft?" Neil set the chisel back down on the truck's tailgate.

"Not the chisel so much as the footprints and tire tracks."

"Where?"

"Everywhere." Little José indicated the ground near them and up the slope.

Neil took in all the people and vehicles and groaned inwardly. Any trace of those footprints and tire tracks was probably eradicated by now. Why hadn't Jake called Neil first before storming out here and bringing three-fourths of his family with him.

The three-fourths, he promptly realized with another glance at the slope, that included Carolina.

His scribbling momentarily faltered.

"This is private property," Gary interjected. "No one comes up here who doesn't work for the ranch."

"What about neighboring ranchers?"

"They have no reason. And the fences are diligently maintained. We can't afford to have our guests coming in contact with stray cattle."

"You rent out ATVs, right? Could any of the guests have come up here?"

Concentrating required all Neil's effort. Carolina's pale yellow jeans and green trench coat made her hard to ignore.

"These trails are too dangerous and off-limits," Gary said.

"Not everyone obeys the rules."

"I suppose." Gary adjusted the knob on one of the lanterns. The flame caught, then glowed brightly. Up at the mine shaft, flashlight beams zigzagged over the ground and on the rock walls.

"So, after you found the chisel and noticed the footprints and tire tracks, you went searching for the mine shaft?"

"I didn't know what I was looking for at first," Little José explained, "only that someone had been here. I followed the tracks up the hill. Once I got close enough, I could see the hole hidden behind a pile of brush. They didn't do a very good job camouflaging it."

"Or they were in a hurry because you surprised them," Neil suggested. "What did you do after you found the shaft?"

"I radioed the ranch. Reported my location and what I'd found."

"I drove straight out here as soon as he told me," Gary said. "Then I called Mr. Tucker. He told me to contact you."

R.J. had done his job. He'd rounded up the family and was bringing them down the hill.

Jake stopped briefly at a white truck then made straight for Neil. "Sheriff Lovitt."

"Mr. Tucker. Do you have any idea who might have done this?"

"None at all." He didn't hide his anger well. "But whoever they were, they had access to some fairly sophisticated equipment."

"Why do you say that?"

"Marks on the rocks. They might be using hand tools now,

but the shaft was originally excavated with a high-powered drill. The experts will be able to tell us more."

"Experts?"

"I've contacted the Arizona Geological Society. Asked them to send out a crew."

"Call them back." Neil wrote furiously in his notebook. "Tell them to wait until someone from CSI contacts them and gives them the go-ahead to proceed. In fact, no one is to go within a mile of this mine shaft without permission. Is that clear?"

Jake nodded curtly, not liking being put off but complying. "I wonder how much gold they've found so far, if any." The question seemed to be directed at himself rather than Neil.

"Maybe the crew from the Geological Society can tell you once they've examined the mine." Neil wrote down a reminder to have someone research places in the state that purchased or processed unrefined ore.

Jake raked his fingers through his hair, his expression showing shock and disbelief.

Neil had seen the same look on countless victims during his career. "Did you have any idea there was gold on your property?"

"No."

"Yes." Carolina stepped forward, hugging her arms to ward off the increasing chill.

Even if Neil wanted to, he couldn't ignore her any longer. Whenever she got within visual range of him, everyone and everything else disappeared. It had been that way from their first encounter.

"Those are just local legends." Jake sounded irritable.

She lifted her chin. "I disagree."

Neil almost smiled. Was there no one who intimidated her? He was instantly reminded of their conversation in the hospital cafeteria, and his fledgling trust in her increased a tiny fraction. He could see her having no reservations whatsoever about defying her boss. And since nothing had surfaced about him or his late wife on the radio, in the newspapers or around town, it appeared she'd kept her promise.

For now anyway.

"What legends?" he asked.

"These mountains were heavily prospected about the time of the Civil War and until the late 1880s," she explained. "Nobody ever struck it rich, but enough gold was found to generate rumors of a mother lode. It's not unreasonable," she added when Jake heaved a tired sigh. "Remember that strike they found outside of Payson twenty…twenty-two years ago?"

"Not really. I was away at college."

She huffed. "Well, I do."

"How much gold did they find?" Neil asked.

"Quite a bit. In the tens, if not hundreds of thousands of dollars."

In today's market, that amount could easily be doubled.

"Have you had the area tested?" Neil asked Jake.

He shook his head. "Gold fever had long since died by the time our grandparents bought the land and built the ranch. Not that our grandfather believed the rumors."

"But Grandma Ida did," Carolina said.

"That's true." The young woman interrupting them looked too much like Carolina to be anyone other than her sister. "She took us once to the Rim County Museum when we were kids. They had this old treasure map on display. A family in town had donated it after finding it among their deceased father's belongings. Grandma showed us where the ranch was on the map and laughed, saying she should get Grandpa to dig for gold."

Neil's glance traveled up the slope to the mine shaft, nearly obscure now in the dark. "I'd say someone else believed the legends, too."

"Or they have the map," Carolina said.

He turned to face her. "Is it still on display at the museum?"

"I have no clue, I haven't visited in years."

Neil underlined the words *map* and *museum* in his notebook.

"You can't seriously believe there's a connection," Jake said.

"People are illegally mining for gold on your property, Mr. Tucker." Neil felt compelled to point out the obvious. "No one would undertake such an operation without being reasonably confident it's going to pay off."

His observation was followed by a round of silence. He used the lull to finish up his notes.

"Hey, Jake," Carolina's sister said, her voice bright with excitement. "We could be rich. Did you ever think about that?"

Chapter Five

While the Tucker and Sweetwater family members mulled over the ramifications of what a potential gold strike might mean to them, Neil went with R.J. to inspect the mine shaft, a process that required a good half hour. When they were done, he radioed the station. The evening dispatcher took down the information he gave her, assuring him she'd contact CSI the moment she hung up. As there was no evidence of a homicide, he didn't expect the investigators to make an appearance until morning, when they had sufficient light to see. In the interim, Neil and R.J. would secure the crime scene to the best of their ability.

"You willing to stay overnight?" Neil asked R.J. "I don't want to take a chance whoever did this comes back." Neil would have volunteered, but Carmen had midterms this week and couldn't babysit Zoey past ten o'clock.

R.J. shrugged. He was a home boy, born and raised in the Payson area. "Won't be the first time I've spent the night in the mountains on the lookout for bad guys."

Neil was grateful the young deputy didn't appear to hold any grudges. He'd been with the department longer than Neil and might have resented not being appointed acting sheriff. The same couldn't be said for all the deputies, and their not-so-subdued grumbling had reached Neil's ears.

He would have to address the problem eventually before it

escalated. Perhaps Sheriff Herberger might have some advice for him. Neil wasn't egotistical or career hungry and had no qualms about asking for help when he needed it.

"I'll send Willie to break you around dawn," he told R.J.

"Be sure he brings a thermos of coffee."

"He doesn't drink it."

"But I do." R.J. grinned.

"You want a doughnut with that?"

"Doughnuts are for city cops. Out here, we have burritos with our coffee. Ernesto's opens early. He can stop there."

"I hope you're carrying a roll of antacids."

"Sissy."

One by one, the family members left, none of them willingly. Neil understood. If his property had been violated, he'd want to stay and protect it, too.

He was shutting the back of the Jeep when his personal cell phone abruptly rang. Unhooking it from his belt, he flipped open the phone and verified the caller ID. His heart rate increased when "unknown" flashed on the small screen. Only very few people had this number—Zoey, her babysitter Carmen, the elementary school, his parents and his late wife's parents.

Had Carmen changed carriers again? He put the phone to his ear. "Sheriff Lovitt."

There was no answer. Only the dull, crackling sound of an open line.

"Hello, Sheriff Lovitt," he repeated, then more firmly, "Who's there?" He was immediately reminded of the threatening phone call from the other day.

A series of beeps sounded, and the line went dead.

He snapped the phone shut. Quickly changing his mind, he dialed his house.

"Everything's fine," Carmen told him when he'd asked about Zoey. "She's watching TV. You want to talk to her?"

"In a minute. Has anyone called the house tonight?"

"Yeah, right before you. Like thirty seconds. I thought when the phone rang again it was them calling back."

"Who was it?"

"They hung up."

"What did the caller ID say?"

"Unavailable. I know I'm not supposed to answer when that happens but I forgot."

"Just be more careful next time." Neil's free hand closed into a fist. Two blocked calls within a minute, one to his private cell and one to his home. He didn't believe it was a coincidence and decided to have Mary Twohorses check his phone records in the morning. "I'll be home in an hour. If they call again, ask for their name and get in touch with me right away."

"Sure." Carmen's tone reflected the nervous anxiety he'd no doubt instilled in her with his brusque questions. "Here's Zoey."

"What's up, kiddo?"

"Daddy, when are you coming home?"

"Not till after you're asleep, I'm afraid."

"Again?"

"Sorry." Zoey's disappointment was no greater than his. Reading her a bedtime story was a ritual they both looked forward to every night. Unfortunately, Zoey would have to get used to him not being there. For a while, at least. Until Sheriff Herberger returned to work. "But I'll come in and kiss you good night."

"Promise?"

"Cross my heart."

She went on to tell him all about the Disney DVD Carmen had brought with her, and for a moment, Neil's world was perfectly right, devoid of unknown callers, dissension among his deputies and fear that his daughter would learn the truth about her mother's death and blame him.

Carolina came over shortly after he'd disconnected, giving him reason to suspect she'd been waiting for him to finish. The cool evening breeze had left her hair in an attractive disarray that he found very appealing. Then again, was there anything about her that didn't appeal to him? She attempted to brush a wayward strand from her eyes, only to have it fall back into place.

He was instantly and unwillingly charmed.

"Hi," she said.

He could sense her trepidation and resisted reassuring her with a friendly comeback. For one, he was on duty, investigating a crime. For another, she was a distraction he could and *should* avoid. Lastly, he still wasn't comfortable with where he stood with her. If the story about his wife broke locally, his career could be in danger. But Neil cared far more about Zoey and the potential emotional impact on her.

On *them*.

If she wound up hating him… He refused to consider the possibility.

"Good evening, Ms. Sweetwater."

"Oh, we're back to that."

"Can I help you with something?"

The lanterns had been extinguished in preparation of everyone leaving. Only a three-quarter moon remained to illuminate the site. Shadows played across her face, adding a hint of mystery to a woman who already mystified him on many levels.

"I was thinking…" Her voice trailed off.

"Yes."

"I'd be happy to take you to the museum and show you the map. If they still have it, that is. If not, I might be able to locate the original owners. I'm sure my mother and uncle remember them."

"Thank you. I appreciate the offer. But I'll have to decline."

"You aren't going to check it out?" She drew back in surprise.

"Yes. But we have procedures. One of my deputies or an officer from the Payson Police Department will likely be following up on leads. Not me."

"The Payson Police?"

"Local agencies work together when crimes cross jurisdictions."

"I see." She wavered.

He wondered why she didn't leave. "Do you have something else on your mind?"

"The stories about prospecting in these parts are really interesting." A hint of annoyance infected her voice. "Despite what Jake says, they may have a bearing on our illegal mining problem. We could meet, and I could tell you the stories in detail. At, um, the station, of course. Not for a meal or anything. Unless you wanted to eat," she ended in a rush.

Neil paused. "Are you asking me out, Ms. Sweetwater?"

She evidently found her courage and answered strongly and confidently, "Yes, I am."

For a brief second, he contemplated saying yes. The idea of going on a date with Carolina, just the two of them, was appealing. But he couldn't accept for many reasons, most of which wouldn't make sense to her.

"I'm honored. Really, I am."

"That sounds like a no." She swallowed, the only visible sign that his rejection had hurt her.

"Sorry."

A horn beeped. "Be right there," she hollered over her

shoulder. To Neil, she said, "Is it because of my job? I told you, I refused the assignment."

"Carolina…"

"I like it better when you use my first name."

She smiled, and his resolve weakened, not that it was ever strong where she was concerned.

"The problem is your job, but also mine."

"Yours? How so?"

"It's complicated."

"Try me."

He was tempted. Good judgment, however, prevailed. "It won't make any difference."

"How do you know?" She stepped forward. No more than a matter of inches, yet it was enough to change their positions— or was it the atmosphere?—from casual to intimate. "Look, there's something between us, don't bother denying it."

He didn't. They'd both have to be blind or naive not to notice the sparks that went off like tiny rockets every time they were together. "Trust me, you're better off with someone else." He started toward the door of the Jeep.

The horn beeped again. Carolina's sister was growing impatient.

"Wait, Neil." She spun around and cupped her hands to her mouth. "Go on without me. Sheriff Lovitt is taking me home."

"Carolina." This time, his voice was stern.

"You have to drive right past my cabin to leave the ranch. Well, practically." She didn't wait for him to answer and dashed around the Jeep to the passenger side.

Neil opened his door. She was already in and buckling her seat belt. The one remaining vehicle with her sister had left and was bumping up the nearby slope. If he didn't take Carolina home, R.J. would have to when Willie relieved him.

Recognizing defeat when it stared him in the face, Neil climbed in behind the steering wheel, hoping he wasn't making a huge mistake.

"TAKE THE LEFT FORK," Carolina said.

Neil shot her a sidelong glance. "That's not the way we came." Neither, he was sure, was it the way the other vehicles had gone.

"I know a shortcut. The trail's a little rough, though. If you're worried—"

"I'm not." He downshifted.

"I didn't think so."

He couldn't see her face in the Jeep's dark interior, but he felt relatively certain she was smiling.

"Careful, the next slope drops off sharply." She tightened her hold on the grab bar and gave an excited "Whee" when they exploded down the other side.

Great. One more thing to like about Carolina Sweetwater. His deputy R.J. could take a few lessons from her when it came to the art of off-road driving.

The noise, the bouncing and the level of concentration required to steer the Jeep hindered any meaningful conversation until they reached the outskirts of a maintenance yard and the main dirt road that led through the ranch. They continued driving, guided by lights peeking out from between the trees, evidence that many of the guests were still awake in their cabins.

"How much farther?" he asked.

"About a quarter mile. Keep going."

Hiking and ATV trails veered off in various directions. Carved wooden signs tacked to trees proclaimed the various trail names. Cute names, like Bear Tracks and Fox Cub and Juniper Berry. One name stood out.

"Did I read that right? Carolina May?"

She nodded. "Grandpa Walter named a trail for each of us grandkids."

A stone monument stood at the base of the next trail. They were going too fast for Neil to read the entire rectangular brass sign.

"Hailey…?"

"Hailey Beatrice Trail. For my cousin, Jake's sister. She died in a horse riding accident almost four years ago."

"I'm sorry."

"Thanks. She was a great person. We all really miss her. Jake especially. They were close, and he took her death pretty hard."

Neil sometimes forgot that he wasn't the only person to ever suffer the loss of a loved one.

"There." Carolina pointed ahead. "Go right."

If not for her, he would have missed the turnoff. The lack of lights, denser foliage and narrowing of the road indicated this part of the ranch was less traveled.

"We're here."

Neil slowed the Jeep and parked.

The one-story structure, set slightly back from the road, had the appearance of a home rather than a guest cabin. Flowers lined the stone walkway leading to a porch complete with a swing on one end and a pair of wicker rockers on the other. A white picket fence straight out of *Little House on the Prairie* surrounded the property, and a rooster weather vane sat atop the peaked roof. Along the side of the yard was what appeared to be a vegetable garden.

At first, the quaint country charm of the place seemed in contrast to Carolina's sophistication. But on closer inspection, Neil decided she fit right in. He could easily picture her planting tomatoes in the garden or curled up on the porch swing, a book in one hand and a glass of lemonade in the other.

It was also the kind of place where he could picture himself, sitting next to her on the swing, her bare feet in his lap, the two of them lolling away a lazy Saturday afternoon.

An unexpected noise penetrated Neil's thoughts. "Is that a dog barking?"

"My sister's French bulldog. Actually, it's her husband's. The dog came with him as part of the deal. I'm babysitting while they're on their honeymoon."

"Should you let her out?"

"Give her a second. I had a doggie door installed, and she's still getting used to it."

Carolina had no sooner spoken than a compact black bullet traveling close to the ground came tearing out from behind the house. The dog stopped at the gate and proceeded to raise the alarm, letting everyone within hearing distance know an intruder had invaded the premises.

Carolina rolled down her window. "Quiet, Belle, it's me."

The dog immediately went from barking to scratching at the gate before plunking her behind down to wait.

"Is she okay there?"

"The gate's latched, she can't get out. Besides, she enjoys being outside. Give her a minute, and she'll find a hole to dig or a cricket to chase."

On cue, Belle trotted off, her nose glued to the ground.

"Zoey wants a dog." Neil had no idea why he said that.

"They're a lot of responsibility. I haven't had one since I left home for college, and I'd forgotten how much work's involved."

"But you like the dog." He could tell from her voice.

"Yeah, I do. If I weren't so busy, I'd get one of my own."

"I try that same argument about being too busy on Zoey, but she doesn't understand."

"Kids are tough to fool."

"She also wants a horse."

"I did, too, at her age."

"But you had a place to keep one."

"True."

"She's going to start riding lessons next week. Here, in fact. Her school's offering an afternoon program."

"I know. This is something new for the ranch. We've had such good luck partnering with the Horizon Adult Day Care Center, the family decided to try a similar program with the elementary school."

"She's excited. I'm not sure how but she twisted my arm and convinced me to buy her a pair of pink cowboy boots." He leaned back in his seat. Being with Carolina was effortless. He'd felt that way about her since their double date.

Being with her, however, was also tempting, and Neil knew he should leave before his impulses won out and he did something stupid.

Except he didn't leave.

"Would you like to come in for a minute?" Carolina tilted her head at an engaging angle.

"Thanks, but I can't. I need to get home. Zoey's babysitter has to leave by ten." The excuse was a weak one, given it wasn't quite eight-thirty.

"Please. It's important."

"I don't—"

"This isn't easy for me."

It wasn't for him, either. The desire to touch her was powerful—link fingers, nuzzle cheeks, inhale the scent of her windblown hair. He didn't care what so long as there was intimate contact.

"We really should talk."

"One of my deputies will contact you."

"Not about the illegal mining."

"Okay."

No, not okay. Neil wasn't sure he wanted to pick up where

they'd left off at the mine site when he'd rejected her dinner invitation. Sitting with her in the dark, close enough that he could feel the seat shift every time she moved, he might not have the willpower to say no if she asked him out again. His imagination drifted to the porch swing, the two of them sitting with her long, bare legs draped across his lap.

Wait, wasn't that feet? When did she go from wearing jeans to shorts?

He fumbled for the keys.

"I went out on a limb, suggesting we meet for dinner," she began softly. "I think that entitles me to know the real reason you turned me down."

"I told you. It's my job."

"Is there a conflict of interest because I'm the victim and you're heading up the investigation?"

"There could be."

"The investigation won't last forever."

"No." With any luck, the culprits had left a piece or two of incriminating evidence behind in their haste to leave when Little José surprised them.

"And besides," Carolina continued smoothly, "we're both adults and more than capable of separating our work from our personal lives."

"Maybe *you* are." Even that small admission was more than Neil had intended.

"I'm flattered," she said, a smile in her voice.

He scrubbed his face, the bristles of his five-o'clock shadow scratching his palms. This was going from bad to worse, and the only way he could see to prevent disaster was to level with her. But that would require he let down his guard.

Neil hadn't done that with anyone since Lynne. Not even with Zoey, and she was the center of his universe.

"I guess that's my cue to go," Carolina said with a hint of

disappointment. Unbuckling her seat belt, she reached for the door handle.

His hand covered the small space separating them and gently took hold of her arm. He had no idea what he'd done until he felt the cool fabric of her coat sleeve beneath his fingers.

"What?" She turned. Her gaze darted to his hand before connecting with his.

Insane for sure, but his grip on her tightened.

"What?" she repeated more softly.

Neil had always been a man of action, not words. That the right thing to say should fail him now was no great surprise.

"Stay." He swallowed, took a breath. "Please." He had to explain. Make her understand.

She remained rigid. "Give me one good reason. You've already hurt me once. I can't handle a second time."

He nodded and let go of her arm.

But before she'd moved so much as an inch, he raised his hand to her cheek and cradled it tenderly.

"How about this for a reason?" he said, and drew her toward him.

CAROLINA RESISTED Neil's advances, and he let her. After all, she was right. He'd hurt her.

Besides, he was still buckled in and unable to maneuver more than a few inches. If they were going to finish what he'd started, it was entirely up to her.

"You're infuriating," she told him.

No argument there.

"And you don't play fair."

"Guilty as charged." To prove her point, he traced the outline of her ear with his index finger.

She gave the tiniest, softest of moans.

It was probably just as well the seat belt restrained him. No telling what he'd do otherwise.

"Sometimes you can be a real jerk."

Ouch! That was harsh. His finger stilled. He'd obviously underestimated her anger and should let her go. But not before he apologized.

"Carolina—"

She leaned across the seat divider, cradled his face in her hands and brought his mouth to within inches of hers. "But mostly, you're incredibly sexy, and I'd never forgive myself if I didn't take advantage of the moment."

For several long seconds, nothing happened. Neil remained perfectly motionless, suspended midway between heaven and hell, afraid she'd start kissing him, afraid she wouldn't and that he'd miss out on what was promising to be one of the best experiences of his life.

Finally, thank God, she ended his torture—or was that began it?—by sliding closer and melting into him.

Neil's arms went around her, settling into place as if they belonged there. What started out as a hesitant exploration quickly built into an explosion of supernova proportions they were both at a loss to contain. She tasted exquisite, felt incredible and wreaked the kind of havoc on his senses that could send him hurtling toward the edge in a matter of minutes.

He knew he should put a stop to her while enough of his brain function remained for him to think straight.

In the next instant, she angled her head, slipped her hand inside his jacket and laid her palm over his pounding heart.

After that, thinking ceased altogether. There was only Carolina. How could he have gone so long without this? Her mouth tantalized his, her scent enveloped him, her heat invaded every inch of him. He must have been crazy.

No, he *was* crazy.

Leading her on was wrong. Unfair. Unkind. He had to… had to…

He clasped her by the shoulders to gently ease her from him. She must have misread his intentions for she deepened their kiss, taking him to a place he hadn't been for years.

Four years, to be exact.

Neil had dated and kissed women since coming to Payson. Pecks, mostly. On the cheek or sometimes the lips. But not like this mind-blowing, can't-get-enough-of-her kiss that pushed his resolve to its very limits.

She saved him from a total loss of control by pulling back. "Well, so much for my sister's theory," she said, and slid back into her seat.

"What theory?" His heart continued to hammer, and perspiration lined his brow. He wiped the dampness away with the back of his hand and might have unsnapped the buttons of his jacket except for fear he'd be sending her the wrong signal.

"She had the nerve to suggest I only ask out guys I'm not interested in." Obviously made of stronger stuff than him, she showed no evidence of waging an emotional war with herself.

"You were trying to prove them right?"

"Yes," she purred.

"Okay." The dig gave him a much needed reality check. It also served to remind him just how vulnerable he was where she was concerned. "I guess after all the things I said to you earlier, I deserved that."

"You goon." She laughed and rolled toward him, wrapping a shapely leg around his. "Don't you get it?" Clutching the front of his jacket, she lifted her face to his for a quick kiss that was nonetheless reeling. "I'm interested in you, Sheriff Lovitt, and have been from the moment we met."

All his silent reasoning in the past five minutes hadn't sobered him as much as what she'd just said.

The dog, bored with being left to her own devices, appeared at the gate and resumed whining.

Carolina groaned. "She's worse than having a mother who flashes the porch light. I really should go and feed her before she dumps over the garbage can. I didn't know anything so little could get into so much trouble." She sifted her fingers through the hair at Neil's temples. "Come inside with me. Never mind," she said, before he could answer. "I forgot Zoey's babysitter has to leave."

He'd disappointed her again. And once started, he couldn't stop himself from doing it over and over.

"It wouldn't make any difference."

She stilled. "Because?"

"I can't go inside with you. Can't go to dinner with you. Can't be alone with you."

"I see." She visibly stiffened.

"Before you storm off," he said, "please listen to me." He exhaled slowly. "I care about you."

"Really?" The tilt of her head implied he had a strange way of showing it.

"I do. Much more than I should." Here was the part where he could use a coach to help him choose what to say. "Lynne's dead because of me."

"It was an accident."

"Call it whatever you like, my lack of judgment triggered a chain of events that ended with her dying. Afterward, I promised myself I wouldn't put the people close to me in danger. It's the reason I sent Zoey to live with her grandparents. It's the reason I took a job in a small town when I couldn't stand being separated from her."

"How is shutting yourself off from a relationship with me going to protect me?"

He blinked away an image of Lynne in a pool of blood. "If we're not together, you're less likely to wind up in the path of a killer's bullet."

"There are no killers lurking in the shadows, Neil," she said, her voice gentler.

"There could be."

"This is Gila County. Hardly anything bad ever happens here. You said so yourself."

"Ten years ago Sheriff Herberger's house was torched by the brother of a man he'd arrested."

"That's one incident. And if I remember correctly, no one was home at the time."

"One incident is all it takes."

"You're willing to risk Zoey's life."

"Yes, and I live in constant fear for her safety. It's gotten worse since I was appointed acting sheriff. I'm suddenly more visible. More people know who I am. Who my daughter is." He laid his head against the seat back and closed his eyes. "Zoey's my only child, and I'm her only parent. I tried giving her up. My life wasn't just incomplete without her, it was unbearable."

"But you can give me up." Disappointment more than anger tinged her voice.

"Today I can." He turned to look at her. In the semidarkness, her features were soft and sweet and achingly lovely. "What scares me is that if we keep seeing each other, keep doing what we just did, I won't be able to give you up. Ever."

"It's hard to tell, but did I hear a compliment in there somewhere?"

"You did."

She studied him, her gaze critical. "Are you sure you're not overreacting just a little?"

"Not everyone in Payson supported the county commissioner's decision to appoint me acting sheriff."

Her eyes widened. "Has something happened?"

"I received a minor threat the day of the interview, and someone's been calling my home and private cell phone and hanging up. The same type of thing happened after Lynne died."

"Pranks?"

"Not all of them." A chill coursed through him. "Twice I was accosted outside my home. The perpetrators got away."

"What about Zoey?"

"Fortunately, she was at her grandparents' then. I'll do whatever's necessary to safeguard her until Sheriff Herberger's well and I can go back to being just a deputy."

Or back to hiding in a hole, as Neil referred to it during those rare moments when he was honest with himself.

"What about us? Can we...keep doing what we just did when Otis is well?"

He didn't respond immediately.

Her laugh this time was bitter. "Boy, I just keep setting myself up, don't I?"

"I can protect Zoey better than I can you. She's five and has to do what I tell her to."

"And I don't," Carolina stated.

"You *won't*. You're very much your own person. I like and admire that about you, but it makes protecting you damn near impossible."

A range of emotions flickered across her face. Neil began to think he was finally getting through to her.

"I don't believe you, Sheriff Lovitt, and I'm getting tired of your excuses."

Wrong again.

"Carolina."

She wrenched the handle beside her, flung open the door and stepped outside. "Sounds to me like you're trying to protect yourself. Not Zoey and certainly not me."

"Even if you're right, which you're not, it won't change anything. I have a duty and a responsibility."

She sniffed. "I need a man who isn't afraid to get involved."

"I understand."

"I think you'll regret this one day." She slammed the door shut and walked away.

He didn't have to wait that long. He was already regretting it.

Chapter Six

"Don't think just because your family's guest ranch is one of our sponsors you can pick and choose your assignments."

"That's not it, Ward." Carolina sat with her hands on the table in front of her, trying not to twist the tennis bracelet on her left wrist. She'd returned the diamond engagement ring Lonnie had given her but kept the bracelet he'd surprised her with their first Christmas together.

Not all her experiences with her ex-fiancé were bad. Just the final ones.

After the other day, when she'd informed Ward she'd rather not do the story on Neil, her boss had blown up, but promptly cooled down. Then today, he'd called her into the small conference room, demanding she accept the assignment on Neil. His annoyance came across like an afterthought, as if he were following a protocol he didn't fully support.

But even with the lack of intensity, his reproof still caused her extreme discomfort. For an awkward moment, she was that little girl who'd dumped the entire container of fish food into the aquarium. Apparently she hadn't matured much since then.

"I'm sorry to disappoint you, Ward, but I can't help feeling a negatively slanted exposé on Neil would hurt him and his daughter unnecessarily. Not to mention adversely affect the people of this county and their safety."

"How so?"

"Targeting Neil, creating problems for him, could distract him and compromise his ability to perform his job."

He crooked an eyebrow at her. "That's a stretch."

"Not a big one. We don't know how he'll react. Cops have that adrenaline thing going."

Talk about a stretch. Neil was the epitome of cool. Except when he'd kissed her. He'd been hot enough to blister the Jeep's leather seats.

"Are you willing to risk your job for him?"

Ward's question gave her a start. Vi had asked Carolina the same thing, and she'd believed then her boss wouldn't threaten her with unemployment.

Wrong again.

"Yes," she said, gulping.

Reporters had ethics, right? Like Woodward and Bernstein. They'd gone to jail to protect their source.

Comparing herself to journalistic legends didn't take the sting out of potentially losing her job.

"I'm not going to fire you, Carolina," Ward said evenly.

Whew! That was a relief. She tried not to go limp or burst into tears.

"But there will be repercussions."

"I understand." She'd prepared herself for a formal written warning.

"You can forget about any more roving assignments for the foreseeable future."

While not entirely out of the blue, the announcement still hit her hard. Step two of her life-redirecting plan was to advance her career. This was a huge setback.

"And you'll be put on probation for ninety days."

Correction, a brick wall.

"Isn't that a little extreme?" she choked out.

"Not for insubordination. Read your employee manual."

She didn't reply. How could she with a giant, painful lump lodged in her throat?

What would Neil say if he knew all she was going through for him? Would he change his mind about dating her?

Doubtful.

If she didn't like him so much and sympathize with his position, she'd resent him.

"I'm sorry, Carolina," Ward said.

"Me, too." She nodded.

"If it were up to me alone, I'd let you off with just a verbal warning."

Because he did sound genuinely sorry, she risked her fragile state and looked at him. His face showed a strain she hadn't previously noticed.

"Are you okay?" she found herself asking.

"Fine. Why?"

"You just seem...a little distracted."

He busied himself with her personnel file, which lay open in front of him.

"You're not usually so nice," she blurted.

"Nice?" He glowered at her. "I just put you on probation for ninety days."

That was more like it.

"Is there anything else?" she asked.

"No." He didn't glance up.

She started to rise from the conference table. Being confident she'd done the right thing was some solace but not enough. She really had her heart set on being a roving announcer. It was hard seeing her dream put on indefinite hold.

Unless...

Inspiration was a beautiful thing.

She sat back down.

Ward lifted his head and appraised her curiously. "Forget something?"

"Did you hear about the illegal mining operation they found on the ranch this weekend?"

"No." His expression quickly went from surprise to interest.

"It was in yesterday's paper."

"Erica and I were in Tempe over the weekend, visiting Len. We didn't get back until late last night."

Their eighteen-year-old was a promising freshman quarterback, attending Arizona State University on a full athletic scholarship. Ward couldn't be prouder. Neither could his wife, who tooted her stepson's horn as loudly as his father did.

"What happened?" He pushed Carolina's personnel file aside.

"One of our hands was riding the trail and found a mine shaft. Turns out, someone's been excavating for gold on our property."

"No fooling!" Ward listened attentively as Carolina filled him in on the details. "What are you going to do?"

"Nothing at the moment. We're stalled until the authorities complete their investigation. That could take weeks or even months."

"Do they have any idea who's behind it?"

"Not so far."

"I'm amazed. Really. There hasn't been any significant gold discovered in this area for decades. It's quite a story."

"That's kind of my point." She readied herself for the pitch she was about to make. "You said yourself you wanted to raise the quality of our newscasts. Well, here's our chance."

"Explain." His pen beat a rhythmic tap on the tabletop.

"This story has far-reaching ramifications. It's not just a matter of a crime being committed. Apparently, there's gold in our hills. It could impact the entire town, if not the county."

His eyes flickered.

Bingo, she thought with a smile. "Gold fever. Imagine the

scores of new listeners we can win over by covering this story. We could run daily updates. Include local lore and stories from the mine strike twenty years ago." She reminded herself to check with the museum about the map.

"What strike was that?"

"Up by Quail Butte. Southeast of town." She frequently forgot Ward wasn't a native of Payson. "I'll copy the old newspaper clippings for you."

"If I agree to let you cover the story, will your family give the station exclusive rights?"

"No one will be allowed on the ranch unless they work for KPKD."

"And no interviews except to us?"

"Absolutely."

"What do you want in exchange?"

"We can negotiate."

"Free advertising for the ranch?"

"That's a start."

He stared at her. "You want to be in charge of the story."

"Yes."

"I did just tell you to forget about any future roving assignment."

"There is that."

"I can put someone else on the story."

"Then I can't guarantee KPKD exclusive rights. Besides, I'm the best candidate."

"Are you?" He sat back, evaluating her.

"It makes perfect sense." Riding the momentum she'd already started, Carolina ticked off the reasons on her fingertips. "The illegal mining is on my family's ranch. I grew up in Payson and am familiar with the town's history. I have previous journalism experience and a connection with the local law enforcement."

"Sheriff Lovitt," Ward said.

"Actually," she said, swallowing to clear her voice, "I was referring to Sheriff Herberger. He and my uncle are old friends."

After the fiasco with Neil Saturday night, any "connection" she'd had with him was severed. Every time she recalled asking him out, she cringed with embarrassment. When she thought of their kiss, her cheeks flamed. And remembering his final rejection made her want to kick the closest piece of furniture or break down and cry.

So far, the love-life portion of her redirecting plan was one big fat disaster. She'd move past Neil and focus her attention elsewhere, except no one else remotely interested her.

Not to the degree he did and not after the other night.

Neil had amazing kissing skills. Angels-singing, earth-moving, heart-going-pitter-patter kind of kissing skills.

Stop thinking about him, Carolina silently scolded herself.

Hadn't he been crystal clear about not wanting to get involved with her? She might consider his so-called promise to himself stupid, but he was committed to it, and she wasn't desperate enough to grovel.

"Sheriff Lovitt would be a better connection," Ward said, "and he likes you."

Yeah, for all the good it had done her.

"Sheriff Lovitt is very much by the book," she said, "and he's already refused to cooperate. I doubt I can get much information from him."

"Use your feminine wiles."

"He's immune."

"You know?"

"I've tested the waters. He's not biting."

"It's Sheriff Lovitt or no deal," Ward said decisively.

"What?" Carolina sat up as if poked with a sharp stick.

"You can be in charge of the story but only on the condition that you cultivate your connection with Sheriff Lovitt."

"Why? Sheriff Herberger is—"

"He's on medical leave. Not actively involved in the investigation."

Oh, dear. This wasn't what she'd planned.

"You want the assignment or not?"

"Yes. I do."

"Excellent." Ward smiled as he stood. "I'll tell the station's legal counsel to draw up the contract."

"My family will have to review it first," Carolina mumbled. She was still in a bit of a daze. "I don't have the authority to sign without their consent."

"Fine. In the meantime, you can move your stuff into Frank's old cubicle."

"Really?"

Her own cubicle. One she didn't have to share with the evening traffic director. Her spirits immediately rose, only to plummet as she remembered the tradeoff—working closely with Neil.

Not a problem. She could, she assured herself, be a professional.

And just who did she think she was kidding?

"WHAT ARE YOU doing here? I thought you had a meeting with your boss this afternoon."

Jake's surprise was legitimate. Carolina seldom visited the ranch's riding stables. Hailey, Jake's sister, had been the serious rider in the family, a position his oldest daughter, Briana, now held. Most afternoons, the teenager was either practicing her barrel racing, working with her high school equestrian drill team or giving riding lessons to the special-needs individuals from the Horizon Adult Day Care Center.

"I got off a little early," Carolina said.

"Really? Why?"

"That's sort of what I wanted to talk to you about."

She had caught Jake just as he was coming out of the barn office. He was probably consulting with Gary Forester about ranch business. While the family met and voted on major issues, day-to-day operations were Jake's responsibility.

"I had an interesting meeting with my boss this morning. Told him in no uncertain terms that I wasn't comfortable doing the story on Neil." They both began walking toward Jake's truck, which was parked in front of the main corral.

"How did that go?"

"Not as bad as I anticipated."

"Excellent!"

They reached the truck and, by unspoken agreement, leaned their backs against the sidewall to carry on their conversation.

"Yeah, I guess."

"You don't sound too happy."

"I thought Ward would be tougher on me." She flipped up the collar of her coat to ward off the breeze. In a matter of days, their Indian summer had ended and the weather had turned chilly.

"And you're disappointed?"

"No, confused. He's been acting a little weird lately—not like himself. He gets mad over the most minor incidents then turns around the next day and blows off something that would normally send him through the roof."

"Count yourself lucky you got off as easily as you did."

"There's a little more to the story."

"And a little more to your visit here, I'm betting."

Carolina grinned sheepishly.

Of all his Sweetwater cousins, she was closest to Jake. Maybe because she was most like his late sister Hailey. Not in looks or horsemanship but in personality. Hailey had also liked to defy convention. Carolina hoped the soft spot Jake held for her would sway him into going along with her plan.

"What do you need?" he asked.

"Why do you automatically assume I need something?"

"Carolina." His tone was reproachful.

He definitely knew her too well.

"All right, here's the thing. I've tentatively agreed for the family to give KPKD exclusive rights to the illegal mining story in exchange for me being put in charge of it."

"I see."

As she explained the details of the tentative deal she'd struck with Ward, Carolina observed Briana from the corner of her eye. The teenager led a group of about a dozen very young children from the barn into a small corral. At first, Carolina assumed the children were offspring of guests at the ranch. As they came closer, she saw they all wore identical lime-green ball caps and name tags on the front of their jackets. Bells went off in Carolina's head. These children were participants in the after-school riding program.

Which meant one of those squirming and squealing munchkins was Neil's daughter.

"Do you think the family will have a problem with it?" she asked Jake after she'd told him everything.

"I'm not sure we should talk to anybody about the mining. Not until we know more, which could be a while."

"We wouldn't be providing details of the crime itself as much as the effects of the illegal mining from the victims' standpoint."

"Won't talking to the media hinder the investigation?"

"Or help it. Whoever's behind the mining is probably local or has local connections," she said, quoting the newspaper report. "The more people are made aware of what's going on, the more likely someone will report suspicious activity to the Silent Witness Hotline."

"Yes, but—"

"And people have a right to know what's happening in their community." Carolina liked the sound of that and would use the same argument on Neil when she attempted to enlist his aid.

"The free advertising with KPKD's sister stations across the southwest is good," Jake reluctantly concurred. "Will your boss let us choose when commercials for the ranch air? Three o'clock in the morning won't reach our targeted market."

"We'll simply make that a condition of our agreement."

Jake continued to weigh the pros and cons with her for several minutes. Carolina half listened, the noise and commotion in the corral diverting her attention to her niece and the class she was conducting. She tried to pick out which one of the eight girls was Zoey. From this distance, and with their identical ball caps, it was impossible.

"I think a family meeting is in order," Jake announced.

"I figured you'd say that. We have to decide right away. I told Ward I'd have an answer for him by Wednesday."

"That's cutting it close."

"The illegal mining is breaking news. We have to act quickly."

"I'll call you later. Let you know what time's convenient for everyone tomorrow."

She pushed off his truck and gave him a brief hug before heading to her car. After a week in the body shop, it looked as good as new. The fender bender might never have happened.

Instead of getting into her car and driving away, Carolina meandered over to the corral. Briana was using Big Ben, the very old, very gentle mule that belonged to the Horizon Adult Day Care center, to introduce the children to equine basics.

On closer inspection, it wasn't so difficult to pick out Zoey. At least, Carolina was fairly certain the girl with the bright pink cowboy boots and saucy ponytail poking through the hole in the back of her ball cap was Zoey.

A young woman who didn't look much older than Briana wore the same ball cap as the children, identifying her as part of the after-school program. If she was supposed to be in charge, Carolina had her doubts. The woman was clearly terrified of large animals, even one as gentle as Big Ben. She visibly trembled as she brought the students up in pairs to pet the mule. Luckily, Briana's experience extended beyond horses to children. She was a babysitter extraordinaire and a wrangler on trail rides.

Zoey was in absolute awe of Big Ben, and he seemed equally enamored of her, lowering his head and nuzzling the hand she extended.

"Very good," Briana said. "Did you all see how she kept her hand flat so Big Ben wouldn't nip her?"

Beaming at the praise, the little girl returned to the group.

Carolina continued to watch the children from her place at the corral fence, debating whether she should stay or go. If she remained much longer, she'd risk running into Neil when he came to pick up Zoey. Unless he sent his daughter's babysitter, in which case, Carolina would miss him. She wasn't certain which scenario she preferred.

If KPKD and her family came to an agreement, she'd be given the illegal mining story, and have no choice but to solicit Neil's cooperation. Given that they hadn't exactly parted under the best of circumstances the last time they were together, the prospect of seeing him again triggered a bout of nerves. Better to wait another day to conduct what could be a delicate conversation with him.

Having made up her mind, Carolina started to leave.

"Who wants to sit on Big Ben?" Briana asked.

"Me, me!" Small hands flew like crazy into the air.

Except for one.

"Teacher, teacher, I have to go to the baf-room."

"Can you wait?" the young woman asked. "We're almost done."

"I gotta go now." The little girl jumped up and down to emphasize her need.

"Me, too." This time it was Zoey.

"Sorry. You're going to have to wait. I can't leave the other kids alone. It's against the rules."

"But this is a 'mergency," the first little girl pleaded, her face contorted.

The young woman glanced around, visibly flustered. "I guess we can break for a little while so all of us can go."

A chorus of voices rose in protest.

"Hey, Aunt Carolina," Briana called out. "Have you got a minute?"

Carolina halted. "Uh...sure."

"Can you take these kids to the restroom?"

"I don't know," the teacher said uncertainly, tugging on the strings of her hoodie.

"Don't worry. She's my aunt and one of the owners."

Carolina changed direction and walked toward the gate. "Taking riding students to the restroom just happens to be on my list of duties."

"Okay," the young woman relented.

Good thing. She'd probably have a riot on her hands otherwise. The remaining students were arguing over which one would be the first to sit on Big Ben. Briana handled them with the kind of patience that kept her phone ringing off the hook with babysitting requests.

The two pint-size cowgirls met Carolina at the gate.

"Come on, follow me," she said, directing them to the barn where the public restrooms were located.

They beat the crowd by a few minutes. A group of guests

were just returning from a trail ride. Their horses, all of them old pros, trotted into the open area in front of the barn, eager to be home. Carolina listened to the guests' excited banter as she held open the restroom door so the first girl could go in.

Which left her standing outside the door and alone with Neil's daughter.

She was sure the girl was Zoey. Besides the pink boots, she had Neil's serious expression and the same dimple in her chin.

"Hi, I'm Carolina. What's your name?"

"Zoey."

All doubts were put to rest.

"I hear you like horses."

The girl peered up at her, intrigued. "How do you know that?"

"I'm a friend of your father's."

"Oh." Zoey scratched the toe of her boot in the dirt.

"Do you like school?"

"It's okay."

Was Zoey normally shy or just around strangers?

"I work at the radio station. I interviewed your dad last week. Did you hear it? He mentioned you."

"No, I wanted to listen but Daddy said I had to go to school."

"That's too bad. If you want, and your dad says it's okay, I can get you a copy of the interview and you can listen to it at home."

"Really?" A smile blossomed on Zoey's face.

"Sure."

Without warning, a banging noise sounded from inside the restroom.

Carolina knocked on the door. "Are you all right in there?"

"Yes," came a muffled reply.

She waited, and when no other noise followed, shrugged off the incident. "I like your boots."

"Thanks." Zoey bent and brushed away some dirt from the top of one.

Their conversation was stilted and probably wouldn't be occurring at all if Carolina wasn't trying so hard. She considered herself good with little girls, thanks to having so many nieces. She wondered if Zoey's shyness was a result of being an only child, having no mother, or just her personality.

Come to think of it, her father wasn't much for casual chitchat, either.

When he chose to, however, he could make up for any lack of words with action.

The restroom door abruptly banged open, and the other little girl emerged. She started to race back to the corral.

"Hey, wait! Don't go."

"She never listens," Zoey said with very adultlike exasperation.

Carolina was torn between chasing after the little girl or remaining with Zoey. In the next instant, the dilemma was solved when the child reached the corral gate and the supervisor signaled Carolina.

"Okay, your turn," she told Zoey, who stepped into the restroom with all the enthusiasm of Dorothy entering the witch's castle.

After giving the interior a thorough once-over, she turned around and shut the door—only to come charging out three seconds later, squealing and hopping from foot to foot.

"There's a tarantula in there!"

"Are you sure?" Carolina was flabbergasted. The huge spiders were indigenous to the area but reclusive, normally choosing to avoid people. "Where?" She poked her head inside the restroom.

"In the corner. Behind the toilet." Zoey's voice quaked.

Carolina bent cautiously to have a look. Despite their size, scary appearance and bad reputation, tarantulas were relatively harmless. That didn't mean she was in the mood for a close encounter with one.

"I don't see it."

Zoey tiptoed up beside Carolina and pointed. "There. On that silver thingie."

The valve? Carolina squinted. A spider with a body no bigger than a pinhead clung to a small iridescent web.

"That's not a tarantula."

"You sure?" Zoey squeaked.

"Positive. Tarantulas are this big." Carolina demonstrated with her hands. "That spider's only this big." She pinched her thumb and index finger together.

"My daddy says I should be careful of spiders."

"And he's right. You don't always know which ones are dangerous. But this one isn't."

"I don't have to go to the bathroom anymore."

"You want me to get rid of the spider?"

"Don't kill it!"

"I won't, I promise. I'll just ask it to leave."

"You can do that?"

"Watch me." Carolina waved her hand in front of the spider. It immediately scurried off, disappearing into a crack in the wall. "See. All safe."

"What if it comes back?"

"It won't. Not till you're gone. I promise."

Zoey looked skeptical but need apparently won out. She went back into the restroom, leaving the door open a tiny crack. A few minutes later, she came out, still wary. By then, several people from the trail ride had joined them.

"Did the spider come back?" Carolina asked.

"No."

The bottom of Zoey's pant leg had become caught in her boot.

"Here." Pulling her aside so the others in line could get by, Carolina stooped and straightened it. "Can't have you looking like a greenhorn."

"What's that?"

"Someone who doesn't know anything about horses."

"But I don't know anything about horses."

Zoey was so earnest, Carolina had to laugh. "But you will soon." They started walking back to the corral.

"Daddy!"

Before Carolina had a chance to react, Zoey sped off. Neil stood by the corral fence. What Carolina saw next strummed her heartstrings like nothing else had in a long, long time.

Neil, wearing an expression of pure joy, scooped his daughter into his arms and hugged her as if it had been months rather than hours since they'd last seen each other.

Zoey was one lucky little girl to be the recipient of such obvious love.

"Hey, pumpkin pie. How are you?" He set her down and held her away from him so he could look at her.

"I'm going to ride a horse. Wanna watch me?"

"You bet."

She skipped off, then came to a sudden stop. "There was a big, scary spider in the bathroom. Carolina asked it to leave and it did." With that, she was gone.

Neil turned to Carolina. "Hi."

She knew it was his daughter that had put the besotted smile on his face but she basked in its radiance anyway, forgetting for a moment the awkwardness and injured feelings of their last parting.

"Hi yourself." She walked over to join him. They both leaned their arms on the corral railing to watch Zoey with Big Ben.

"You asked a spider to leave?" Neil appeared skeptical.

"It's a long story and not nearly as exciting as Zoey made it sound."

"That's a strange-looking horse."

"He's a mule. The differences are lost on young children."

"I think they're lost on me, too."

"Half horse, half donkey."

"I'm not going to ask how that works. I don't think I want to know."

"I'm sure Zoey will tell you after Briana explains it."

"I can't wait."

Zoey finally got her turn to sit on Big Ben. Neil and Carolina both shouted encouragement and clapped when she was lifted off. Cars pulled into the open area, parents arriving to collect their children. Guests from the trail ride continued to mill around the stables, watching the hands unsaddle the horses and put them up for the night. The place had turned into a hive of activity.

"I should probably get going," Carolina said.

"I'm sorry about the other night."

Neil's comment was out of the blue. She waited a moment to gather her thoughts before responding.

"Apology accepted."

"To be clear, I'm not sorry about kissing you."

Neither was she.

"I wish I'd handled things better. Not hurt you." His hand involuntarily opened and closed around the railing. "I'd like us to be friends."

She let that trite platitude pass for the moment. "Good. Because I may need your help in the near future."

"With the investigation?"

"Sort of. My boss is putting me in charge of a new story. If we can work out the details."

"What story?"

"The illegal mining operation." She drew on her courage, which was in shorter supply than usual these days. "And you're my connection in the law enforcement agency."

Carolina was pretty certain she'd struck Neil dumb, but then he answered her, just not the way she expected.

"I accept."

Her jaw dropped. "You'll do it?"

"No. I accept your dinner invitation."

"I'm...confused."

"You're right. We need to talk. Is Thursday okay? I'll pick you up at your place. About six okay?"

He didn't wait for her reply, merely strode off to get Zoey.

Chapter Seven

At Neil's knock, the dog—he couldn't remember its name—started barking. Carolina promptly opened her front door, and her smile flickered for only the briefest of seconds.

"You brought Zoey!"

"I hope you don't mind."

"Of course not."

"You have a dog." Zoey squealed and knelt down on the porch floor to welcome into her lap what had to be one of the ugliest dogs he'd ever seen. "What's his name?"

"*Her* name is Belle. And I'm just babysitting. Until tomorrow. After that, she's going back home to my sister's house."

"She's so cute," Zoey cooed between dog kisses.

That was a matter of opinion. With a short, squat body, a severe underbite and round bat ears, the dog wouldn't win any beauty contests. Zoey, however, didn't appear to notice.

"I want a dog."

"Me, too," Carolina said.

"Daddy says we're too busy."

Belle flopped down and rolled onto her back. Zoey got the hint and began to scratch the dog's pudgy belly.

"Maybe you can come with me to the animal shelter and help me pick out my new dog."

"Really?" Zoey beamed.

"Are you serious?" Neil didn't beam.

"I'm sorry," Carolina said, meeting his gaze. "I should have cleared it with you first before asking her."

"No, I meant, are you serious about getting a dog?"

"Yeah. I'm tired of living alone."

Her quick laugh didn't cover the trace of loneliness he detected in her voice. For a moment, Neil was taken aback. Carolina had impressed him as being completely satisfied with her single life. Was he wrong?

"I heard the dog pound is overcrowded and having an adoption drive all month long," Carolina said.

"Can I go with her, Daddy? Please." Zoey stood and took Carolina's hand.

They presented a formidable front.

He studied the two of them for a moment, unable to speak. Zoey had formed relationships with women in her young life besides her grandmothers: preschool teachers, mothers of friends, the very nice lady next door. But she'd been relatively shy with them at first, requiring a long period of adjustment before she'd trusted them enough to initiate physical contact. She'd met Carolina briefly at the ranch and was already holding her hand.

On second thought, Carolina had had much the same effect on him. They hadn't been fifteen minutes into their double date when he wanted to trade places with the guy across the table from him.

"I shouldn't have mentioned getting a dog," she said apologetically.

Neil reached out and smoothed Zoey's flyaway hair. "Sure. You can go."

Zoey dropped to her knees again to hug Belle. "Did you hear that? You're getting a new brother or sister."

"That was sweet of you." Carolina smiled at Neil.

He promptly remembered what he planned to tell her

tonight and wondered if she'd have the same opinion of him afterward. Probably not.

"Let me grab my jacket, and I'll be ready to go." She retreated, appearing a moment later with the same green trench coat she'd worn the night he'd been called out to investigate the illegal mining operation. The same night they'd kissed. He could still feel the coolness of the fabric beneath his fingers… and the soft heat of her lips on his mouth.

He tugged at his shirt collar. Bringing Zoey tonight wasn't an afterthought. He'd known he would need a buffer, that being alone with Carolina would test his willpower to its limits.

"Come on, sweetie," he said to Zoey when Carolina stepped outside onto the porch. "The dog has to stay here."

They literally had to pry Zoey and Belle apart. Neither wanted to be separated. Once the dog was safely behind the closed front door, Carolina grabbed hold of both Neil's and Zoey's arms.

"Hurry." She dragged them along with her. "We only have about thirty seconds before she escapes through the doggie door."

They made it in the nick of time. Belle barked goodbye at the gate.

"Where are we going?" Carolina asked when they were in the car and pulling away from her cabin.

Zoey pressed her face to the rear passenger-side window and waved at Belle. The dog stood with her front feet on the gate, a forlorn expression on her cute-ugly face.

Seems Zoey was as quick to make friends with the dog as she was with Carolina.

"Pickle's Pizza," Neil answered her question, naming a kid-oriented pizza parlor with arcade games and rides. He thought Carolina might cringe at the suggestion.

She didn't.

"I love that place!"

Figured.

Even on a Thursday night, the restaurant was packed with families and children. That was what Neil wanted. More buffers to help him remain focused and not let his thoughts drift to other things. Like how sexy Carolina looked in black jeans. Or the way the dangly gold earrings she wore kept drawing his eyes to her face and the lovely curve of her lower lip. He'd tasted that lip and traced the outline of it with his tongue—

Zoey let out an excited squeal. She'd spotted two of her friends from school at one of the games. Rather than ask Neil to go with her, it was Carolina she coerced into playing skee ball when he handed over a fistful of game tokens.

"Do you mind?" Carolina asked.

"Have at it." He sat by himself to order their pizza.

All around him, children ran, screamed, laughed, played, bickered, cried and made messes. Most of the adults sat at their tables, attempting to converse or enjoy their meal. A few of the heartier ones like Carolina joined the fray, monitoring the younger children or playing games.

He watched her and Zoey, the two of them enjoying themselves, and wondered again why his daughter had taken so quickly to Carolina. Even Carmen, whom Zoey adored, had required a "warming up" period that lasted several days.

Was it his fault? Had he sheltered Zoey so much he'd inadvertently instilled in her a wariness of new people? That wariness could protect her from harm, but too much, and she could become socially isolated.

Maybe her instincts were right on target, and she sensed that Carolina was someone she could trust, someone who wouldn't hurt her.

He could learn a thing or two from his daughter, he supposed. His trust in Carolina was still tentative, though growing with each passing day.

And now she wanted his help with her story on the illegal mining. No doubt he owed her a favor for keeping his past under wraps and for being so kind to Zoey. Refusing her request would be hard.

It was also necessary.

Neil had worked diligently and sacrificed much to get his and Zoey's lives where they were today. Quiet, safe, normal, secure. Not just physically but also mentally and emotionally. Carolina threatened to disrupt their perfectly ordered lives.

She could give him reason to care for her, had done it already if he were completely honest with himself. And the idea of loving again, of gambling with another person's life and possibly losing her, terrified him.

NEIL'S HEAD SHOT UP when Carolina appeared in his line of vision. Before he could issue an invitation, she sat down beside him at the picnic-style table. "I don't think I've ever seen you out of uniform."

"I'm off duty."

"New York Yankees fan, huh?" Her glance strayed to his T-shirt and lingered.

"Where's Zoey?" he promptly asked, needing his buffer.

"With a friend at the miniature basketball game."

"Did she wear you out?"

"Are you kidding?

"Is that a yes?"

Carolina let her shoulders sag and blew out a breath. "A little."

"You lasted a lot longer than I would have."

"Practice. I come here often with my nieces." She gave him a thorough and considerably longer once-over. "I like it."

"The pizza place?"

She shook her head. "You look good in civilian drag."

So did she. Damn good.

"Not so tough," she added with a grin.

"Don't be fooled by the clothes."

"You forget, I've seen you with Zoey. You have a marsh-mallow for a heart."

"Only for her."

"No one else?" Carolina asked coyly.

Was she a mind reader, too? He wanted to say something witty back to her but his speech center had temporarily shut down.

She laughed and blithely moved on to a new subject, effectively reducing his confidence around women to that of a high school freshman.

"I'm beat. How do you keep up with Zoey all day?"

"I can't. That's why I hired Carmen."

"Smart man."

Casual bantering came easily to Carolina. It would be equally easy to respond to her. Neil needed to shore up his defenses—and fast—if he was to stay on track during the evening ahead.

"Did your family agree to give the radio station exclusive rights to the illegal mining story?" he asked.

She hesitated, then, in typical Carolina fashion, forged ahead. "Yes, they did."

"And did your boss award you the story?"

"Yes, he did."

Neil didn't realize until that moment how much he'd been hoping for a different answer.

"You aren't going to help me," she said flatly.

There went his plan for letting her down slowly. "No."

Before he could elaborate, the pizza arrived. Neither of them dug in. Neil scanned the crowd for Zoey. Finally finding her, he summoned her over to the table by holding up a paper plate with a slice of pizza on it. While he and Carolina waited for his daughter, she dished up two more slices, giving one to him.

For Zoey's sake, Neil wolfed down his pizza. She was already asking too many questions about his restlessness and diminished appetite. The last thing he wanted was for her to pick up on the tension between him and Carolina, who was making a much better show of eating than he was. He figured it was her way of demonstrating to him that his refusal to cooperate with her request didn't bother her.

"What kind of dog are you going to get?" Zoey asked Carolina around a large piece of crust that was almost more than she could handle.

"I haven't decided. Probably one that was a stray or abandoned and really needs a home."

Carolina and Zoey went on to discuss the merits and drawbacks of various breeds, big versus small, fluffy versus short-haired, purebred versus mixed, cute versus—well, they were all cute according to Zoey.

Neil began to reconsider his plan to wait to get a pet. If his daughter was occupied with a dog, she'd pay less attention to him and the stress that was affecting his mood. Then, when Otis returned to work, Neil's life could resume its quiet routine.

Except for Carolina.

"Can I go play now?" Zoey asked when she was done eating. Pizza sauce was smeared all over her face.

He picked up a napkin and started to wipe her chin.

"Daddy." She grabbed the napkin from him and scrubbed at the sauce. "I'm not a baby."

"Sorry. I forget sometimes."

She fled the table with only half the sauce removed but all of his heart.

"She's adorable," Carolina told him. "You're a very lucky father."

"I am." The time had come to be honest. "I had a reason for bringing her with us tonight."

"Oh?"

"I wanted you to see firsthand how important she is to me."

"I never doubted for one second she wasn't."

"I admit, I'm overprotective of her. It comes with the job and being a single parent." Neil pushed aside the aluminum tray with its three slices of uneaten pizza. "Also the circumstances of Lynne's death."

"You're going to have to let Zoey go eventually."

"Spoken like someone who doesn't have any children."

Carolina didn't appear offended by his blunt remark. "You're right. It's not my place to judge or criticize."

"And you're right, too. I will have to let her go one day. But not yet."

"I don't wish to be unkind, but are you sure that isn't your guilt talking?"

"It probably is." Admitting a potential flaw in his thinking changed nothing.

She placed the leftover pizza in a take-out box the server had left on the table for them. "I don't see what any of this has to do with refusing to cooperate with me on the story about the illegal mining. I thought you'd be happy I was given a new assignment."

"The illegal mining operation is no backyard recreation project. You can bet whoever's behind the digging is serious, has resources and is dangerous." The CSI team's preliminary investigation had confirmed Neil's initial findings. "They don't want to be exposed. They don't want to be caught. And there's no telling what action they'll take to prevent either of those things from happening. You could find yourself an unintentional target, caught in the middle or...hurt."

He imagined worse but refrained from saying it.

"People are entitled to know what's going on in their community," she proclaimed passionately.

He'd heard that line before and was immune. "I don't care about the people in this community."

She gave a soft, mirthless chuckle. "That's a strange attitude for the man charged with serving and protecting them."

"Not like I care about you."

That shut her up. For about ten seconds.

"How much?"

She had to ask.

"Too much."

"Then why won't you help me? This assignment is important to me. It's the career break I've been waiting for."

"Because your safety and well-being are more important to me than your job."

"You're overreacting," she insisted. "I'm not in danger."

"You are, just by virtue of being one of the ranch owners. Investigating the illegal mining will triple the risk. I can't, I *won't*, elevate your exposure by helping you with the story."

"I think you're letting Lynne's death affect your judgment."

"Hell, yes, I am."

"We're not dealing with a serial killer here."

He could almost feel the gun in his hand, hear the Delivery Man's shot as it ricocheted off the brick building outside the deli. "That doesn't make the individuals behind the digging any less ruthless."

"Now that the mine's been discovered, I'm sure they've left town. Why would they stick around?"

"Because they live here."

She sat up. "I know that's what the papers are saying, but do you really think so?"

"Yes. There are two aspects to every operation, brains and

money. The money may not be local but the brains are. How else would they know where to dig?"

"Which is even more reason for me to do the story. We have criminals operating and residing among us."

Rather than dissuade her, his argument had fired her up.

"Wrong. If these people know the area, it stands to reason they know you and your family. You're not the only one who could be in jeopardy. What if something were to happen to Briana or one of your other nieces?"

His remark appeared to take at least some of the wind from her sails. "What if I promise to be careful?" she asked.

"It's not that simple."

"Fine." She wiped her hands on a paper napkin and tossed it aside. "I'll just find another connection in the department—or the Payson Police or the Arizona Geological Society."

"Don't be so stubborn."

"Don't be so controlling."

"I'm trying to protect you."

"Right. Because you care about me. Which, let's face it, is irrelevant because you refuse to get involved with me."

"If I did get involved with you, would you turn down the story?" He knew he'd messed up the instant the words left his mouth.

She drew herself up. "Thank you very much, but I don't need to negotiate for a man in my life."

"Sorry." How often was he going to apologize to her? "That came out wrong."

"I'm leaving now." She lifted a leg over the picnic table bench. "Don't worry, I can catch a ride back to the ranch."

"I'll drive you home." Neil also untangled himself from the table, with much less grace than Carolina, and went on the hunt for Zoey. When he found her with some of the boys at the air hockey table, he called her name. She didn't look happy at having to leave her friends.

Swell. Now both his dinner companions were angry at him.

He helped Carolina on with her coat, then Zoey. Neither of them appreciated his efforts.

"Do we have to go?" Zoey complained.

"It's a school night."

"My fault, sweetie." Carolina took hold of Zoey's hand. "I have an early curfew. But I promise to make it up to you."

"How?"

Carolina scrunched her mouth to one side, deliberating. "We could go for ice cream after we finish dog shopping."

"Dog shopping?" Zoey giggled.

They walked ahead of Neil toward the exit, intentionally or unintentionally excluding him.

Frankly, he didn't know how he felt. Part of him was pleased to see his daughter bonding with Carolina. Zoey needed a strong female role model in her life. The other part of him resented the intrusion. He was used to having his daughter to himself. That she should so easily respond to someone other than him left him mildly jealous and, he was reluctant to admit, a tad insecure.

Reality hit him square in the heart.

Like it or not, whatever safeguards he took, his daughter was going to meet and develop meaningful relationships with people outside their small family, including some future young man. Neil could accept that, as long as Zoey loved him and included him in her life. And waited. Fifteen, twenty years ought to do it.

What about him? Was he willing to wait fifteen or twenty years until Zoey was grown and out of the house to have a serious relationship?

Carolina was too vibrant and attractive, not to mention impatient, to hang on for that long on the off chance he'd wise up. Especially when he offered little in return.

Lately, he'd found himself wondering how Lynne would have felt about the prospect of another woman filling her shoes. They'd only discussed how she and Zoey would continue on if anything happened to Neil, a much more likely possibility considering their jobs. Knowing the depths of her love for him and Zoey, he guessed she'd want them to cherish her memory and their years together, but to find someone else who made them happy.

None of that, however, lessened the guilt he suffered over her death or the fear that history would repeat itself with someone else.

With Carolina.

An older couple and two youngsters who looked like grandchildren entered the restaurant at the same time Neil was exiting. He recalled the couple from a vandalism he'd responded to the previous month at their house.

"How are you?" He nodded pleasantly.

They gave him an odd look and a murmured, "Hello."

Neil thought it was a bit strange, but people's reaction to law enforcement officials was often reserved and uncomfortable, even when they had no reason to be nervous.

Carolina and Zoey were already outside, and he quickened his pace in order to catch up with them. Turned out there was no need. They were waiting for him by the newspaper box, chatting up a storm.

In the next instant, that changed. Carolina grabbed Zoey's arm and yanked her away, saying in a falsely bright voice something about finding the car.

Neil's instinct kicked in, and he closed the distance between them in a hurry. "What's wrong?"

Carolina's cheeks had lost all their color. *I'm sorry,* she mouthed, and her eyes darted to the newspaper dispenser.

A stack of the evening edition faced out.

Neil read the headline. A sensation akin to being kicked in the stomach almost brought him to his knees—Acting Sheriff Lovitt Investigated In Late Wife's Death.

Chapter Eight

"Neil!" Sheriff Herberger boomed, ushering Neil inside. "Good to see you."

"Hi, Otis. Hope I'm not bothering you. When I called earlier, your wife said you wouldn't mind the company."

"Are you kidding? A week at home and I'm already going nuts. Driving Patty nuts, too," he said, referring to his wife. "It's going to be a long leave of absence for both of us."

Neil removed his hat, hung it on a nearby coatrack and followed the sheriff into a cozy front room. Despite the older man's obvious good spirits, his step lacked its usual spring, evidence that the recent heart surgery had taken a toll on him.

"Can I get you a cup of coffee or cold drink?"

"Coffee's fine." Neil took a seat in the chair facing the window. The entranceway to the living room was on his left. Old cop habits died hard, he thought as he sank into the soft cushions. The chair's location allowed him to see the room from all angles as well as the street outside.

"Cream and sugar, right?" Otis asked.

"If you have it."

"I'll warn you, the coffee's decaf. Patty won't let me drink anything else."

"Decaf's fine."

Neil would have appreciated the extra kick to his system.

He'd spent half the night tossing and turning or pacing the floor, trying to get that damned newspaper headline out of his mind. The second he'd seen it, he'd been hurled back in time four years ago to a similar headline in another newspaper. That one had nearly destroyed what little had been left of his life.

"Sit tight, I'll be right back," Otis said, leaving Neil alone.

The decision to visit the sheriff had come to him about two in the morning during one of his numerous trips to the kitchen. It would probably be an exercise in futility, but he wasn't one to sit around doing nothing. He needed to find out who had leaked the story about Lynne to the newspaper and why. The sheriff might be able to help. If nothing else, he was someone Neil could confide in without having to hold back or watch what he said. That alone would be a relief.

While he waited for Otis, he removed his jacket and studied the room. It was packed with enough antiques, old photographs and personal memorabilia for three houses. This wasn't Neil's first visit to the Herberger home since moving to Payson. On those occasions, Otis had recounted the house's long and colorful history as one of the oldest residential dwellings in town.

The house had belonged to his wife Patty's family. Her great-grandfather, a renowned bootlegger and swindler, had settled in the area—some claimed escaped there—from Iowa during the 1910s when prohibition was in effect. The family's lawlessness had ended with him. Future generations went on to become some of the town's most upstanding citizens.

"Here you go." The sheriff returned, bearing two mugs of steaming coffee.

Neil stood, realizing he should have offered to carry the coffee himself. The older man's face was flushed from the mild exertion.

"I'm assuming this isn't a social call," he remarked once they were both seated. "What's on your mind?"

Neil cut to the chase. "Did you happen to see last evening's paper?"

"No. I usually try to read it after dinner but the doctor has me taking a short walk instead, and once I get home from that, I can't stay awake if my life depended on it."

"Here." Neil reached inside the jacket lying across his lap and removed a folded section of the paper. Leaning forward, he passed it to Otis.

Removing a pair of reading glasses from his shirt pocket, the older man snapped open the newspaper. "Well, I'll be damned," he said, then proceeded to read in earnest. When he was done, he handed the paper back to Neil, his features reflecting his disgust.

"You didn't know they were going to run this?"

"Hell, no!"

"Sorry if I offended you," Neil said. "You're well connected in town. I thought someone might have mentioned it to you."

"I've been existing in a cocoon since the surgery. I think folks are afraid of upsetting me and giving me another heart attack."

"I probably shouldn't have come by."

"No, no. I'm glad you did. I'm not an invalid." He shook his head. "But back to this," he said dismally. "Finding out about you isn't hard. Anyone with access to a computer and the Internet could pull up information."

"Do you have any idea who'd want to do that and why?"

"Have you made any enemies since coming here?"

"There are a few individuals who don't like me."

"It goes with the territory."

"Some of them are on the county payroll."

His bushy eyebrows shot up. "Just what in the Sam Hill is going on?"

"A couple of the deputies aren't happy about my appointment." Neil filled the sheriff in on the grumblings he'd heard and the string of dead phone calls.

"Do any of them dislike you enough to try and damage your reputation?" he asked when Neil was done.

"I'm not sure. You know them better than me. What do you think?"

"I can see one or two of them getting their noses out of joint. Hank especially. He's been with the department almost as long as me. But to go so far as to employ petty scare tactics and launch a smear campaign?" He jerked his thumb at the newspaper in Neil's hand. "I don't know. Strikes me as kind of underhanded, and Hank's more of the in-your-face type."

Neil agreed. "If you hear from him or any of the guys, let me know."

"Count on it."

"And if you have any advice on how to handle things, I'm willing to listen."

Their visit continued with Otis giving Neil the benefit of his vast experience. He, in turn, brought Otis up-to-date on what had been happening at the station and in the community. Besides the illegal mining at Bear Creek Ranch, there wasn't much. Their conversation centered mostly on the current status of the investigation. Neil could almost feel Otis's desire to get back to work, and he sympathized. Men like him didn't cotton well to inactivity.

"What about Carolina Sweetwater?" Neil asked.

"What about her?"

"You're friends with her family. Would she have leaked information about me to the newspaper?"

"I don't see why she would."

Neil wasn't about to explain the complexities of his

relationship with Carolina to the sheriff. "Last week, her boss at the station ordered her to do a story on me."

"Why?"

"It was right after my appointment. He apparently considered me newsworthy."

The sheriff scratched behind his ear. "I don't recall hearing anything on the radio."

"Carolina refused to do the story."

"You don't say?"

"My question is," Neil said, "do you think she would have leaked the story to the newspaper?"

"I think a better question is, why would she do it now? What would she have to gain? If she wanted to expose your past, she'd have agreed to do it for KPKD."

Neil had come to the same conclusion last night when he'd been sitting in his dark kitchen, unable to sleep.

"Carolina may be a bit of a flirt," Otis said, "and date a lot of men, but don't let that fool you. She's as solid as they come. Honest as the day is long."

Neil didn't know her like the sheriff, but he tended to agree.

"Shame about her and that ex-fiancé of hers. The company he worked for shipped him to Mexico City for a two-year assignment. She wanted to go with him but her parents pressured her into staying. Mainly because the family trust doesn't allow for owners to live outside the U.S."

Though tempted, Neil refrained from asking any further questions. The sheriff might become curious as to the reason for Neil's interest, and he wasn't ready to explain.

Fortunately for him, the sheriff was in the mood to talk. "Rather than wait two years for her, the bum dumped her. Broke her heart."

Neil couldn't imagine any man in his right mind dumping Carolina.

Then again, hadn't he, in a roundabout way?

No, there was a difference between refusing to enter into a relationship and breaking one off. Especially an engagement.

"That's too bad." Neil purposefully kept his response neutral.

"It changed her, but then, I suppose those things do. Patty thinks that's why Carolina dates so much. She's trying to forget how much the SOB hurt her." The sheriff scoffed. "But after five years, you'd think she'd have gotten over him."

Neil knew firsthand some things were just too painful to ever get over.

"Another cup of coffee?"

"Wish I could. I have to hit the road."

Otis walked Neil to the door and clapped him on the shoulder. "Stop by anytime."

"Rest up."

"That's all I do." He rubbed his protruding belly. "And eat rabbit food. That damn doctor put me on a diet, too. There's no end to his torture."

Back in his cruiser, Neil turned on the radio and adjusted the volume to low. Since he was the last one to drive the vehicle, the radio was already set to KPKD. At the end of the commercial, Carolina's voice came on. She was giving her final traffic report for the morning.

Neil turned up the volume and listened. How any woman could sound sexy reading a list of current traffic conditions, he didn't know. But Carolina did. Was every man in listening range thinking the same thing as Neil? For a moment, he pictured a townful of men in their cars or at their desks, all of them fantasizing about kissing Carolina.

Neil didn't have to fantasize; he could simply remember.

And it was killing him.

When she finished, Rowdy Rodgers bantered with her for a few seconds before promising to see her on Monday.

She and Neil had hardly spoken last night on the drive to her home from the pizza parlor. He'd been too shocked to talk. A hundred possibilities had swirled around in his head, and a hundred new worries and fears constricted his chest. All he'd known was that he needed to rush Zoey home and, if possible, get his hands on every copy of the newspaper before people read them.

He'd only succeeded on the first count.

Carolina had sensed he didn't want to talk about the headlines in front of Zoey and occupied his daughter by asking her about dogs and school and horseback riding and favorite flavors of ice cream.

Was it a clever ploy? Despite what Otis had said about her honesty, Neil needed to speak to her in person about the leak.

At the next intersection, he went straight instead of turning right. The radio station and Carolina were one short mile down the road. When he arrived in the parking lot, he immediately spotted her blue PT Cruiser. She was still at work.

He sat in his vehicle for several minutes, debating whether to go inside or wait for her to come out. By the time the third person walked past, looking at him nervously, Neil made up his mind and went in.

"I'm here to see Carolina Sweetwater," he told the receptionist behind the large and cluttered front desk.

She almost broke three long, glittery fingernails in her haste to buzz Carolina.

"Is there somewhere we can talk?"

"My cubicle's this way."

"In private."

Carolina suppressed the small frisson of worry coursing

through her. She had no idea what to make of Neil's unexpected appearance. Obviously, it had something to do with the article that had appeared in last night's paper and the follow-up one this morning. But since she hadn't tipped off the reporter, a fact she'd stressed as strongly as possible during their brief moment alone at her front door, there had to be another reason behind his visit.

His sole response to her claim of innocence had been a tight-lipped nod, which could be interpreted multiple ways. He didn't believe her, or he believed her but was angry at whoever had leaked the story. He believed her but didn't want to discuss the matter with Zoey nearby, which could account for his visit this morning. *He didn't believe her.*

It was hard not to come back to that.

"Management is using the conference room for a meeting," she said, conscious of Marcie the receptionist's avid interest. "The only other semiprivate rooms are the break room, which is like Grand Central Station, or the supply room."

The idea of being shut in a crowded, messy supply room with Neil struck Carolina as terribly sitcom cliché. It also thrilled her. She might be mad enough at him to spit nails, but that didn't change her attraction to him or her desire to repeat the searing kiss they'd shared.

Under different circumstances, of course. Not when he was standing across from her, glaring from beneath the brim of his cowboy hat.

She imagined him in the dress blues of the NYPD. The khaki uniform of the Gila County Sheriff's Office suited him just fine but so would the other. No denying it, those shoulders of his would do justice to any jacket.

"Is there someplace else we can talk?" he asked.

"Afraid not."

Adrian, the techie who'd invited Carolina on a date a few weeks ago, cruised by with the office manager. Both cast not-so-discreet glances at Neil. Clearly they'd read the newspaper article or heard about it.

Neil ignored them, though the muscle in his jaw twitched, showing Carolina he wasn't immune. "Are you off work yet?"

"Normally, I would be," she said. "But I'm working late on the illegal mining story."

That went over like a lead balloon.

"Can you leave?" His request came out like an order.

She resisted rolling her eyes and said to Marcie, "Let Ward know I'm going out for lunch."

"You got it!"

Carolina could just picture the station's phone system lighting up like a Christmas tree as the entire staff buzzed about her leaving with Neil.

They headed down the street rather than toward the parking lot.

"How about Ernesto's?" he asked, putting on his sunglasses.

"For what?"

"Lunch."

"That was just an excuse I gave Marcie."

"So, you're not hungry?"

"Are you?"

From behind the dark lenses, he gave her a look she could only guess at. "Let's walk. There's a little park on the corner."

"Fine."

Carolina was acutely aware of the attention they garnered from pedestrians and occupants in passing cars. Even those people who didn't recognize Neil were probably wondering why a woman was strolling along the street with a uniformed lawman.

The park brought back memories. It wasn't far from the

Rim County Museum, and Carolina's grandmother had often brought her and her sisters here on their visits to town.

"How's this?" Neil indicated a vacant bench beneath an oak tree, its leaves deep in the throes of changing color.

"Can we sit over there in the sun?" She tugged on the sleeves of her sweater. "I forgot my coat."

"Take mine." He removed his leather jacket and, before she could protest, draped it over her shoulders.

Warmth from his body instantly engulfed her.

He took her elbow and led her to the bench.

"Won't you be cold?" she asked, her voice ridiculously high-pitched.

"I'm from New York. Our summers are colder than this."

"Did you grow up in the city?"

"No. Schenectady."

Because the bench was small, they sat close together. Above them, birds flitted from branch to branch, occasionally swooping to the ground to peck for food.

If Carolina and Neil were dating or lovers, the setting would have been perfect. He'd probably slip an arm around her, and she'd rest her head in the crook of his neck. Their hands would reach across their laps, fingers entwining—

"I didn't move to New York until I enrolled in police academy."

The vision, which was sheer madness anyway, disappeared in a small poof.

"Is that where you met Lynne?"

"No. It was much later."

"Were you on a case together?"

"I didn't bring you here to discuss Lynne," he said more gently than she would have expected.

"I know. I'm stalling." She toyed with the hem of his jacket. "How bad is the backlash from the articles?"

"Bad." He didn't elaborate. "And it will only get worse."

"Maybe not."

"Trust me. I've done this before."

"I didn't leak the story to the newspaper. I swear it."

"I believe you."

"You do?" His revelation pleased her.

"You have no reason. If anything, you'd have done the story for the station."

"Well…" She flashed him a guilty grimace. "I could have done it out of revenge when you refused to cooperate with me."

"You're not that type."

This revelation also pleased her. Whatever differences they had, he trusted her. At least when it came to keeping her promises. "How's Zoey taking it? Or haven't you told her yet?"

"I haven't, and I'm not going to."

"Are you sure that's wise? What if she hears about it from one of the kids at school?"

"Kindergarten kids aren't interested in me." He tapped the toe of one boot rhythmically on the concrete sidewalk.

"They might be, if the daughter of the sheriff is in their class. Their parents certainly are."

"I'm *not* telling her."

Common sense told Carolina to drop the subject, but she ignored it.

"You said the other night that you cared about me. Well, I care about you, too. So, I want you to listen to me." She touched a hand to her heart. "Because what I say comes from here. Think seriously about telling Zoey."

"I have."

"Think harder. If you don't tell her and she finds out from someone else, she may feel betrayed and angry."

"She'll feel that way and a lot more if I tell her."

The misery in his voice tore at Carolina. "Maybe not. If you tell her first, you'll have the chance to explain. Prepare her for when she does hear it. There are professional counselors who can advise you if you're not sure what to say."

"She won't understand."

"Don't underestimate her, Neil. She's a pretty incredible kid. She gets it from her dad."

He removed his sunglasses and stared straight ahead, seeing something Carolina couldn't. "I can't take the chance she'll hate me."

For the first time, she realized just how truly scared he was of losing his daughter's affection. Reaching for his hand was an unconscious act. He didn't withdraw when her fingers encountered his.

"Who do you love more than anybody else?" he asked, his voice low and empty of emotion.

"My family. My parents and sisters. And my cousin Jake. He's the older brother I never had."

"You said his sister died in a riding accident. What if you were the one responsible for that accident, and he had no idea. Would you want him to know?"

"He'd have the right."

"What if him knowing would destroy your relationship?"

It was on the tip of her tongue to insist Jake would understand and forgive her. Then she remembered what it had been like four years ago, when he'd wrongly blamed his former brother-in-law for Hailey's death. There had been no understanding and forgiveness in him then. Only later did he gain a new perspective.

"It might take a while, but he'd make peace with me eventually."

"What if he didn't? What if he couldn't stop blaming you for robbing him of the person he loved most?"

That had almost happened. Jake changed only when his anger at his former brother-in-law hurt one of his oldest and dearest friends.

"I'd have to tell him," Carolina said. "I don't think I could live with the guilt."

"You'd tell him just to make your life easier?"

"Not at all! It's…it's…" Would she? "No, I'd be taking responsibility for my actions."

"Believe me. I take full responsibility for what happened to Lynne." Neil's features hardened. "And I can live with the guilt. For the rest of my life if I have to. So long as I don't lose Zoey."

Carolina could see there was no budging Neil, so she changed tactics. "I can do some digging if you want. Try and find out who leaked the story about you to the newspaper."

"Forget it."

"Don't you want to know?"

"Yes, but I don't want you involved."

First the illegal mining and now this. He really was carrying the overprotective act too far. "What harm is there in asking a few questions?"

"More than you know."

She suddenly got it. "You think the person who's calling your home and cell phones is the same person who sicced the newspaper on you."

"I doubt it's a coincidence."

He had a point. Maybe the situation was more serious than she'd realized. "Have you reported the phone calls to…?" Who did the sheriff call when he was the victim of a crime?

"I have." His tone implied he expected few results. "And there's nothing I can do about the articles unless something libelous is printed about me."

Regardless of what he said, she was going to contact her sources at the newspaper, two men she'd dated briefly on different occasions, and see what they had to say.

"I'd better get back to the station." She attempted to withdraw her hand from his.

He held fast. "I'm sorry."

"For what?"

"Everything. Mostly for taking advantage of you that night in front of your house and then telling you we couldn't be together."

"You didn't take advantage of me. I seem to recall it was the other way around."

"I made the first move." His thumb kneaded the inside of her palm. "You're hard to resist, Carolina Sweetwater."

"You appear to be managing well enough."

He turned his gaze directly on her. "I'm not."

Her heart fluttered.

The blue sky overhead, the birds in the tree, the soft breeze playing tag with her hair added to the moment. Kissing him would be a big mistake but she longed to do it anyway.

"Where do we go from here, Neil?" The question left her lips on a whisper.

"I'm not sure."

Her cell phone rang, disrupting the moment. She removed it from her trousers pocket. "Hello."

"Hi. Am I speaking to Carolina Sweetwater?"

"Yes."

"This is Kyle Dunstan, the assistant curator at the Rim County Museum," a cultured male voice said. "I have good news for you. We've located the map you were inquiring about."

"That's wonderful." She felt Neil's eyes on her. "From what you said, I didn't think you would."

"It's in my office if you want to take a look."

"Can I come now?" She glanced at the building across the street. "I'm in the area."

He chuckled. "I'll page the front desk. Give them a heads-up."

"Thank you." She disconnected. "The museum found the map," she told Neil. "I'm heading over."

"So am I."

She couldn't stop him, and if she tried, he might get an injunction or whatever it was called against her. Better to let him accompany her and "cultivate their connection" as Ward had put it. If she stuck close to Neil, she might learn something useful for her story, the first installment of which was due tomorrow.

"Okay, Sheriff Lovitt." She jumped up from the bench. "Let's go."

While she phoned the station to let them know of her change in plans, he radioed the sheriff's department.

"Don't think this means we're working together," he said when they were both done.

"Of course not."

But as they entered the museum and met with the assistant curator, it felt like just that to Carolina.

Chapter Nine

"Counting the gold strike twenty years ago up on Quail Butte," Mr. Dunstan explained, "there have been a total of three significant mining operations in a three-mile radius." He drew an invisible circle on the map with his finger.

Carolina and Neil stood beside the assistant curator, one on each side. The overhead light illuminated even the smallest detail on the map. It also burned into the top of her head and the back of her neck. Another minute of the intense heat and she'd break out in a sweat. Holding Neil's heavy jacket didn't help. She shifted it to her other arm, afraid to lay anything down in the cluttered office in case she damaged an artifact.

"Here's the illegal mining operation." She tapped the map near the center of the area Mr. Dunstan had indicated.

"More like here." Neil's finger lighted a few inches from hers.

"Perhaps they've located the mother lode." Mr. Dunstan's brows lifted. "Wouldn't that be something?"

"Mother lode?" Carolina sputtered the question a scant second ahead of Neil.

"All three mines played out relatively quickly. According to the assayer's records, old newspaper stories and the journal of a particularly colorful young man from Iowa, there were rumors of a mother lode running through the ridge. No one's ever found it." Mr. Dunstan paused for effect. "Not yet."

Carolina immediately conjured up a dozen what-ifs. The most significant one: what if Jake's experts from the Arizona Geological Society reported they'd found gold?

In the meantime, she had a great kicking-off point for her story.

"Do you think whoever's behind the illegal mining operation knows about the mother lode?" Mr. Dunstan asked.

The firm set of Neil's mouth led her to believe he was already considering the possibility.

"Wow" was all Carolina could say.

"Would you like to read the journal?" Mr. Dunstan asked. "It's very interesting and gives an insightful account of life in our budding metropolis during the late 1800s."

"I'll have one of my investigators contact you and make arrangements to pick up the journal and the map," Neil said.

"I'd like to read the journal, too," Carolina said.

"It may be evidence." He glared at her over the assistant curator's head. "Along with the map."

"Not a problem." Mr. Dunstan appeared unaware of any friction between his guests. "I can't release the originals, of course. But I have copies of each. Excuse me a moment, and I'll instruct my secretary to get them for you." He left the room, his rubber-soled shoes falling softly on the hardwood floors.

Neil's boots thumped as he walked to the window then back again to stand beside her.

"I told you, I don't want you involved," he said in a harsh whisper.

"I already am."

"You don't have to do the story on the mining." He inched closer.

She used his jacket as a shield. "Yes, I do."

"No job is important enough to put your safety on the line."

"This isn't just about my job. Someone has stolen from my family and vandalized our property."

"*Attempted* to steal."

"The distinction is a tiny one."

"I understand wanting to help your family."

"I should think so. It's what dictates your entire life. Your every decision. Your relationship with every person you know."

He retreated a step and drew himself up.

"I'm sorry," she said softly. "That was uncalled-for."

"Have you considered what might happen if word spreads about a potential gold strike on your family's ranch?"

"A boom in reservations?" Her tone was more flippant than necessary, but then his had been annoyingly condescending.

"It's possible. But you might also get trespassers, either curiosity seekers or undesirables itching to help themselves to some of your gold. Unless the mine shaft is secured 24/7, trust me, there will be break-ins."

"He's right." Mr. Dunstan returned, carrying a pair of large manila envelopes and two maps rolled into tubes and fastened with rubber bands. "Especially if there is a mother lode. You'll notice there are quite a few instances in the journal of fights over claims. If you haven't already, you might want to check with your attorney."

"I will." Carolina hadn't thought of that.

"He or she can also verify who owns the mineral rights on your land. According to some of the old deeds we have here, the rights didn't always transfer."

Carolina's knees went a little weak.

She needed to call Jake right away. Their grandparents had purchased the ranch over fifty years ago. Who even knew anymore what the original deed said and what rights Grandpa Walter and Grandma Ida had kept or given up?

NEIL SAT at his desk and studied the copy of the map the assistant curator had given him. If it held any secrets or clues, they were hidden to him.

Mary Twohorses entered his office. The distraction wasn't a welcome one.

"Here's the latest report of your phone records," she said.

He didn't ask if she'd read it already. She had. Nothing much at the station slipped past her.

"Anything of value?"

"No. The numbers, there's two of them, are from pirated cell phones."

Neil raised his eyebrows. The person behind the prank calls was going to a lot of trouble to hide his identity.

"And the duration of the calls is too short for the phone company to pinpoint the location."

"It wouldn't do any good anyway. You can bet the user is busy right now obtaining another pirated one."

The question was why? Since taking over as acting sheriff, Neil had done nothing that wasn't routine.

Mary sat down in the chair across from his desk, automatically swinging her long braid over her shoulder to lie in her lap. From old pictures hanging in the break room, she'd been wearing her hair in the same style since the day she started with the department. The only difference was the amount of gray interspersed in the braid.

"What's up?" Neil asked. Mary rarely sat down and only if she had something important to say.

"I know you have to leave soon to pick up Zoey from day care, but I thought you should see this first."

She laid the evening edition of the paper on the desk in front of him, open to the editorial page. There were six letters to the editor, all of them about Neil. He picked up the paper and sat back in his chair. His blood pressure rose with each letter he read.

Neil was the first to admit he had plenty of faults. Being a bad cop, however, wasn't one of them, and having the authors of the letters imply as much angered him to no end. Two of the letters even suggested Neil's appointment be reversed. Not that he'd wanted to be acting sheriff. But there was a huge difference between voluntarily stepping down and being forced to step down.

His gut screamed that there was more going on here. His head, however, cautioned him to proceed slowly. The media onslaught and prank calls were not unlike what he'd gone through during his Internal Affairs investigation after Lynne's death, and he might be overreacting.

Why hadn't this come out when he was first hired on as deputy sheriff?

Because whoever was behind the smear campaign hadn't considered him a threat until now.

He tossed the paper onto his desk.

As much as he hated involving Carolina, maybe he should take her up on her offer and have her check with her sources at the paper. It would also give him a reason to talk to her again. Not that he wanted to start anything, he just wanted to hear her voice. If anyone had asked him last month what part of a woman he found the sexiest, a dozen other attributes would have popped into his head. Since the day he'd responded to the fender bender involving Carolina's niece, a slightly husky, sultrily sexy voice had jumped to the top of the list.

Hearing her on the radio every morning no longer satisfied his craving.

"The last letter isn't so bad," Mary said.

Neil skimmed it. "The person doesn't defend me as much as sympathize with me for losing my wife."

"Sheriff Herberger's contacted the editor and requested they cease publishing letters about you. The paper has a history of supporting him and the department."

"I wish he hadn't. People are entitled to express their opinions." Even if they were ill informed and their opinions half-baked. "It's one of the rights we, as law enforcement officers, protect and defend."

"The editor offered to interview you and run the article on the front page."

"Forget it." No more interviews. The first one with KPKD had caused him enough trouble.

"You might think it through a little more before turning them down."

"It doesn't matter what I say. They'll slant the article the way they choose in order to sell papers." He'd been down this road before. The one interview he'd given after Lynne died had been a fiasco. The reporter took everything he'd said and either quoted it out of context or twisted it to make Neil sound like he'd cared more about the glory of bringing down a notorious serial killer than the lives of his wife and child.

"Your decision." Mary folded her hands neatly in her lap. "It's just that I've worked for this department a long time, under three different sheriffs, including you. In my experience, ignoring problems has never solved them."

"I'm the acting sheriff. This is a temporary job."

"It could be permanent. Otis will retire eventually."

Neil laughed. "I won't run for the position."

"Why not? You'd be good at it."

Because being sheriff would put him and Zoey in the spotlight and elevate the risk to their safety.

"What else?" he asked when Mary still didn't leave.

"Hank's in the break room."

"Okay." The deputy sheriff's shift was due to start soon.

"He's talking to the men about you."

"I take it he's not singing my praises."

"You might want to hear for yourself." Mary's message was clear enough.

Whether he wanted the job of acting sheriff or not, he had it. Neil didn't shirk his responsibilities, and he sure as hell wouldn't let any of his men get away with talking trash about him.

"See you in the morning."

"Have a nice evening." Taking the hint, she stood, a smile on her lips. Mary showing any emotion was a rare sight. He found his own smile lingering after she left.

The break room resembled an efficiency apartment, minus the bed. A kitchenette and dining set occupied one half of the room, a couch, recliner, bookcase and TV the other. Lockers lined the wide hall leading to the room, large enough for each man to stow his personal belongings.

The setup was a far cry from the station where Neil had served back in New York. But as a place to gripe and air disputes, there was no difference. Hank wasn't happy with Neil and anyone within earshot was hearing about it.

"I figured he was hiding something from the start. Now we know."

"Bull crap. You figured squat."

Neil waited by the lockers, listening to Hank bellyache and R.J. jump to his defense.

"Ask Willie if you don't believe me."

"You don't like Neil because he beat your scores."

It was true. Until Neil came to Payson, Hank had held the marksmanship record for the department.

"He got lucky is all," Hank argued.

"Three times? That ain't luck, pal."

"Yeah? Well, I didn't kill my wife."

Neil almost doubled over. Four years, countless accusations, and he still reacted as if slugged in the gut.

"Neither did he." R.J.'s voice took on an edge. "And I'd stop spouting my head off if I were you. Like it or not, he's our boss."

"Not for long," Hank grumbled.

"Is there a problem in here?" Neil stepped out around the lockers.

"Not at all, Sheriff. Me and R.J. was just shooting the breeze before shift starts."

Neil sent Hank a look that the other man would have to be dense not to understand. "Well, if you have anything important to discuss, why don't you do it with me later? Away from the station."

"I'll do that," Hank said evenly.

"I'm looking forward to it," Neil replied.

"Hey, did someone call a meeting or what?" Willie entered the break room. Like Neil, he was heading off duty.

"Waiting on you," Neil said. He briefed R.J. and Hank, letting Willie provide input, then left to pick up Zoey from day care.

As usual, the line of vehicles outside the school stretched to the end of the parking lot. The encounter with Hank had put Neil a few minutes behind schedule, and he had to wait longer than usual. Zoey, never patient to begin with, would be giving the monitor in charge a run for her money.

Instead, his daughter was sitting on the low cement wall surrounding the flagpole and got up only when he pulled alongside the curb. Her backpack dragging on the sidewalk, she trudged toward him, eyes glued to the ground in front of her.

A knot of concern formed in the pit of Neil's stomach. Something had happened. Another fight with her best friend? An unsatisfactory mark on her progress report? Tomorrow's riding lesson canceled?

Her problems might pale in comparison to the ones Neil

had dealt with all day at work, but to her, they were important and therefore to him, too. By the time she opened the cruiser door and crawled in, he was more than ready to listen.

"What's wrong, pumpkin pie? You seem sad."

"Nothing," she mumbled unconvincingly.

He pulled ahead to the exit and turned right. "You sure?"

No reply.

In fact, she said nothing until they were a few blocks from home. He was just beginning to think she might be sick and that he should take her temperature as soon as they got inside when she said, "Some of the kids at school were talking today."

Neil's foot hit the brake and the cruiser came to a stop.

Zoey turned her small face to him and asked in a tiny voice, "Did you shoot my mommy?"

His heart stopped, then started again with a painful thud.

"No, sweetie, I didn't." When had the talk gone from him being responsible for Lynne's death to actually pulling the trigger? "I told you, your mommy died in an accident. A terrible accident."

He pulled to the side of the road before someone rear-ended them. Carolina had warned him of this happening. He should have listened to her.

Zoey's eyes had taken on a distant look, and Neil was suddenly terrified. Did she think he was lying? He reached over, unbuckled her seat belt and pulled her close to him.

"Don't listen to what those kids are saying. They're just being mean."

"Why, Daddy?" She buried her face in his jacket sleeve.

Neil stroked her hair, struggling to come up with a good explanation that his sweet little daughter could understand.

"You know Sheriff Herberger's sick and that Daddy's taking his place until he's well again, right?"

She nodded.

"Not everybody is happy about that."

"Why?"

"They don't think I should have gotten the job."

"Why?"

"Because we haven't lived here very long. Not like the other deputies. Some people don't want a stranger as acting sheriff. They think if they say bad things about me, I'll quit."

"We're not strangers."

"No, we're not. And I'm a good acting sheriff. They'll see that and stop saying lies about me." Or once Otis was back on the job, Neil would no longer be the focus of attention.

"Tell me again about my mommy."

Neil continued to stroke Zoey's hair. She'd been so young when her mother died. She didn't remember Lynne at all. Photographs and stories were his daughter's only connection. He made sure she had plenty of both.

Ignoring passing traffic, Neil recounted for at least the hundredth time how he and Lynne met and how happy they'd been when she was born. When he was done, her mood was greatly improved.

"Would you like to go to Dairy Queen for supper?" he offered on impulse. The leftover fried chicken he'd been planning on serving could wait until tomorrow.

"Yes!"

One of her school friends was at the restaurant. The girl must not have participated in the day's cruel taunting because Zoey was overjoyed to see her. While they played, Neil took out his cell phone and made a call.

"Hello," Carolina answered, a bit warily. "I didn't realize I gave you my number."

"You didn't. I have resources."

"Of course."

He thought he heard a trace of amusement in her voice and was glad. Now wasn't the time to offend her.

"What can I do for you?" she asked.

"I changed my mind."

"Again? That seems to be a trend with you and me."

He didn't comment. She was right, and he was already having trouble keeping his emotions in check.

"I'd like to take you up on your previous offer," he said.

"Which one?"

"To call the newspaper and see if you can find out who's behind the articles on me."

"I already did."

He should have guessed as much. Before he could ask her what she'd found, Zoey came running back to their booth. Her friend's family was leaving.

"I can't talk now," he told Carolina. "Is there any chance you can swing by my house before you head home?"

"Sure, but I won't be leaving for another thirty minutes."

"That's fine." He winked at Zoey and indicated for her to finish up her hot dog. "Let me give you my address."

"No need. I have it."

"You do?"

"I have resources, too, Sheriff Lovitt."

That shouldn't have surprised him.

"ANOTHER GREAT STORY, Carolina!"

"The phones haven't stopped ringing since yesterday!"

Carolina walked down the hall at the station, accepting accolades from her coworkers. Inside, she was tingling with happiness. Her twice-daily reports on the illegal mining operation couldn't be going any better and were generating high ratings.

"Nice job this afternoon, Carolina."

"Thanks, Ward."

"What's on tap for tomorrow?"

"I'm still playing with a particular angle." If everything went well, Neil would give her something new when she saw him shortly. His call had taken her aback, and she wondered what had prompted his change of heart. Perhaps the newspaper articles were getting to him after all.

She frowned, recalling the letters to the editor in yesterday's evening edition. The accusations made were cruel and untrue. She began mentally composing a letter in response.

"See you in the morning," Ward said.

"Bright and early."

She had barely reached the parking lot when Jake called. "What did Howard have to say?" she asked.

Her cousin had contacted the family attorney the moment Carolina advised him of the assistant curator's comments regarding previous claim disputes and mineral rights.

"He's still researching it," Jake answered. "The deed is old and the language unclear. He's contacted a colleague to review the deed. We're supposed to hear back by the first of the week."

"I was afraid of that."

How ironic would it be if the mother lode were on their property and they had no right to it?

"We've had some other news, too. Good and bad."

"Tell me." Carolina switched to her Bluetooth so she could talk on the phone and drive.

"The police called this afternoon. The CSI team is done. I've already contacted the Arizona Geological Society. Their crew will be out first thing tomorrow."

"That is good news." For the family—they'd finally get some answers about how much, if any, gold was in the mine— and for her report tomorrow.

"Unfortunately, the police have nothing further to say on who's behind the illegal mining."

"I'll try and get something out of Neil when I see him shortly."

"You're going out with him?"

"No. Stopping by his house."

"Carolina."

Why did everyone say her name that way, with an unspoken warning tagged on the end?

"It's not what you think. I have information regarding the articles the newspaper has been running on him."

"And you get information from him in return for your reports?"

"Exactly. Purely professional."

Jake's laugh deteriorated into a choking fit.

"Seriously."

"If you say so."

Carolina tried her best to work up a good mad at her cousin. It wasn't easy when she knew deep down he was at least half-right. "We're done discussing this."

"I've got a call on the other line. Hang on."

She drove toward Neil's, pretending the butterflies in her stomach had nothing to do with seeing him and everything to do with her mounting excitement over obtaining information on the illegal mining.

Jake came back on the line. "That was your boss's secretary. The station wants another interview with me tomorrow morning."

"So soon? You just gave them one yesterday."

"It appears they've already heard about the police releasing the crime scene to us."

"That was fast."

"Your boss must have a direct line to the police chief."

"I guess." She turned onto Neil's street. "Hey, I'm almost here. I'll call you later."

"Be careful," Jake said.

"Neil's the acting sheriff. I think I'm pretty safe with him."

"That's not what I was referring to."

"Oh?"

"Don't fall too hard for him, Carolina. He's a good guy but maybe not the one for you."

"I'm not falling for him at all."

Correction, she *was* falling for him, but holding herself in check. So far, anyway.

Clicking off from Jake, she pulled into Neil's driveway. The one-story ranch house had lush landscaping and a spacious front yard filled with a swing set, bicycle and discarded roller skates.

The sun, which had been dropping by degrees during her drive over, was about ready to slip beneath the horizon when she rang the front doorbell.

A moment later, Neil flung open the door.

"Hi, I'm—"

Without any warning, he hauled her into his arms.

Chapter Ten

Carolina wasn't sure what to expect from Neil. A wild, passionate kiss that went on and on? Throwing her over his shoulder and carting her off to the bedroom? Knocking her to the floor a microsecond before a thug lunged at them from behind the bushes?

What she got was a hug.

Not the kind of hug you give someone you haven't seen in ages, but the kind you desperately need when life throws you a curve.

"What's wrong?" she asked, her hands sliding up to circle his shoulders. The hug might not be romantic, but she could still enjoy the sensation of his body conforming ever so nicely with hers.

"Zoey asked me today if I shot her mother."

"Oh, Neil." Her heart ached for him.

"You were right. Some of the kids at school were taunting her."

Carolina pulled back and gazed into his dark brown eyes, brimming with hurt and confusion. "I so hate that I was."

He nodded. "Me, too."

"What did you do?"

"I told her there were people in town who weren't happy

I'd been appointed acting sheriff and they were getting back at me by saying bad things about me."

"Did she believe you?"

"I think so. It's more or less true."

"I'm not sure."

He stepped away and stared down at her. "What did you find out?"

Three seconds apart and already she was longing for his touch again.

"Not a whole lot. My contacts were less than cooperative."

"Let's sit down." He motioned for her to follow him into the kitchen.

"Where's Zoey?" Carolina didn't think he'd want his daughter to hear their conversation.

"At her friend's house across the street. You want anything?"

"A glass of water if you have it."

He got one for each of them while she made herself comfortable at the cozy dining table.

Neil's house was reasonably tidy, the clutter typical of a rambunctious five-year-old and single dad. Although homey and decorative accents were missing, the house felt warm. Carolina's house, which had plenty of homey decor and no clutter suddenly seemed empty in comparison.

"Here you go." He set the glasses of ice water on the table.

"You gonna be all right?" she asked.

He almost smiled. "Why? Do I look that bad?"

"Actually, you do."

His uncharacteristically distracted appearance concerned her. Neil was a rock. The person everyone leaned on in a crisis. Then again, it was easier to be strong for others, and this crisis hit at the very heart of his family.

He made a disgruntled sound and ran his fingers through his hair. It didn't improve his appearance. A small tuft stood up in the center of his head. Carolina found it—and him—endearing. There was something very appealing about a strong, capable man showing his vulnerability.

"Here. Let me." She got up and went to him. "You're making it worse." She smoothed the errant tuft and couldn't resist combing her fingers through the hair at his forehead and temples. "There. Much better."

His gaze locked with hers and intensified. "Thanks."

"You're welcome." Carolina started to move toward her chair but didn't get far. When had he taken hold of her wrist?

Without saying a word, Neil lifted her hand to his cheek and trapped her fingers against his warm skin. The innocent gesture sent a spiral of desire curling through her.

He must have sensed her response for his eyes went smoky.

Her heart raced in anticipation. What now?

In the next instant, Neil let her hand drop and closed his eyes.

Okay, nothing was going to happen. Probably wise, considering.

Carolina continued to stand there for an awkward moment then, with a forced laugh, returned to her chair. "I think you're fit to be seen in public now."

He scowled. So much for showing his vulnerable side. Was he irritated at her or himself?

Since the highly charged moment had obviously passed, Carolina got down to business. The sooner she told him what she'd learned, the sooner she could leave and nurse her injured pride.

"I wasn't able to find out exactly who tipped off the newspaper about your IA investigation after Lynne's death."

He gave a curt nod.

"There's more."

"What?"

"It might be nothing. I could be trying to connect two unrelated dots."

His scowl deepened. "Tell me."

"My contact hinted that the editor of the newspaper decided not to run anything on you after receiving the tip. That he'd researched you and decided the story wasn't relevant."

"What changed his mind?"

"My contact wouldn't say, only alluded to pressure being applied."

"What are the dots you're trying to connect?"

"My contact mentioned that my boss, Ward, and the editor have been talking a lot lately."

"Are they friends?"

"Acquaintances. They're both in the news business and belong to the same professional organizations. But I'd say they're more rivals than friends. Definitely not prone to talking."

Neil appeared to digest the information.

"I wouldn't give it a second thought," Carolina said, "except Ward's been acting strange lately."

"How so?"

"Just not himself. Cutting employees slack when he'd normally bite their heads off, then making a huge deal over nothing." She didn't mention her recent reprimand.

Neil tapped the knuckles of his closed fist on the tabletop. "I agree. I'm not sure there's a connection. But what you said does seem to confirm someone's attempting to target me."

"Do you know why?"

"No." He glanced at her again, his expression devoid of emotion. "And as far as I can tell, I haven't done anything to be a threat to anyone."

"Not yet. This could be a diversion tactic. Insurance against something you might do."

"Perhaps." He sat back in his chair. "I tend to think one of my deputies is carrying a grudge."

"That does make sense."

"I have a few leads I'm going to check out tomorrow."

"Anything I can help with?"

"Thanks. You've done enough already."

"If you change your mind, let me know."

The back door banged open and Zoey bounded into the kitchen. Her face lit up. "Hi, Carolina." She didn't act surprised to encounter an unexpected visitor.

"Hey, kiddo."

"Ms. Sweetwater," Neil corrected.

"Carolina's fine," she said, and winked at the little girl. "We already decided. Zoey can call me Carolina, and I can call her greenhorn."

Zoey giggled hysterically.

Neil rose from the table and pulled her to his side for a brief hug. "What are you doing home? You're not supposed to cross the street without calling me first."

"Casey's mom walked me."

"Okay." He bent and kissed the top of her head. "But next time, call."

"Yes, Daddy." She tried to send Carolina a return wink, only she had trouble keeping one eye open and the other shut.

Carolina was completely enamored.

Neil was blessed to have a daughter like Zoey. No wonder he went to such lengths to protect her. In his place, Carolina would do the same.

Though the idea of lingering appealed to her, she couldn't. "I'd better go."

"When are we going puppy shopping?" Zoey asked.

"Soon. Another week or two." When she was done with the series on the illegal mining. Even if the culprits weren't found, there was only so long she'd be able to ride the tide of excitement. After that, interest would wane. "I'll have some time off work then to spend with the dog."

"Don't forget we're going for ice cream."

"I won't. Oh, wait!" Carolina reached into her purse and pulled out a CD. "Speaking of promises. Here's a copy of your dad's interview." She gave the CD to Zoey. "Your dad said he didn't mind."

"Thank you!"

"Do you have a CD player?"

"Yes, yes," Zoey exclaimed. "Can I listen to it now, Daddy?"

"How about we both listen to it after dinner?"

Zoey stuck out her lower lip but made no further protest.

"Why don't you finish your homework while I walk Ms. Sweetwater to her car."

"Goodbye." Zoey threw her arms around Carolina with such force she almost lost her balance.

"Bye, kiddo." She fought back a wave of unexpected emotion. "I'll call you soon about the dog shopping."

Outside, Neil's expression was unreadable again. Did he not approve of his daughter's budding friendship with her?

"If I'm overstepping my bounds with Zoey, let me know."

"You're not. I'm glad you two are hitting it off."

Okay, apparently something else was bothering him.

"I know I'm probably talking to a brick wall," she said, "but try not to be too upset about the newspaper articles. There might be a mild furor now but it'll pass soon."

No answer to that. Carolina decided to give up.

"Thank you."

He speaks!

"For what?"

"Your help. Being so nice to Zoey. Not pestering me for information on the illegal mining operation."

"Now that you mention it..."

He glowered at her.

"Just one tiny tidbit."

He sighed, long and loud. "Fine. I guess I owe you that. The CSI team was able to lift a number of boot impressions from the site."

"Really!"

"They estimate three men are involved."

"You're not telling me everything." She could read as much in his face.

"That's all you get."

It was enough. "Does the newspaper have this information?"

"Nope. You'll scoop everyone."

"Yes!"

Ward would be delighted. Carolina couldn't help it and threw herself at Neil. He caught her, his arms automatically circling her.

"Whoa!"

"Thank you, Neil. Thank you, thank you."

They both went instantly still as the intimacy of their positions became apparent.

When Carolina would have retreated, Neil held on to her.

"I thought you said this kind of stuff was a mistake," she whispered.

"It is." He lowered his head to nuzzle her cheek and ear.

Shivers danced up her spine. "Then why?"

"Because I can't resist you."

No man had ever said anything so sexy, so disarming, so exciting.

She didn't wait for him to kiss her. Standing on her tiptoes, she raised her lips to his. The resulting explosion was immediate and enough to shake her to her very core. It wasn't, however, enough to jar her loose from his embrace. She clung to his jacket, taking all of him in, letting him fill her senses and stir her arousal.

Wanting more—*much* more—she parted her lips. His tongue swept in and tangled with hers, sending more shivers dancing up her spine. He tasted cool and clean, like the ice water they'd been drinking. The rest of him was anything but cool. He teased and coaxed her with unspoken promises of just how good it could be between them if she gave him the chance to show her.

Their kiss went on and on, which was perfectly fine with Carolina. At some point, his hand slipped inside her coat to capture her waist, eliciting a soft sigh from her. Then his hand moved upward. Higher still. His thumb made a single sweep across the tip of her breast before his palm closed over her.

Wow!

The jolt had both of them springing apart. Not that Carolina objected. His driveway just wasn't the place. That was made more evident when they discovered the neighbor—Zoey's friend's mother?—watching them from across the street.

Fortunately, darkness had settled, so the woman's visibility was limited.

"Howdy, Sheriff Lovitt!" she called, her voice containing a mischievous lilt. "Nice evening."

He groaned.

"Look on the bright side." Carolina escaped his embrace and opened her car door. "At least people have something else to write about you in their letters to the editor."

"Not funny," he grumbled.

She shut the door after getting in and rolled down her window. "That depends."

He braced his hands on the open window and leaned down. "You're dangerous."

"I know."

"Not the way you think."

"I know that, too."

"Be careful."

"Nothing's going to happen to me."

"I don't want to lose you, too."

Carolina was touched.

For a moment, he looked as if he might say more. Instead, he shook his head, straightened and tapped the open window. "See you later."

"Count on it, Sheriff Lovitt." Her voice contained its own mischievous lilt.

CAROLINA EASED through the door of the control booth and shut it behind her. On the other side of the glass, the engineer gave her a thumbs-up. The gesture might have brought a smile to her face if she wasn't already grinning from ear to ear. Her report this morning had gone well, another rocking installment in her series. But that wasn't the only reason for her happiness.

It was Neil.

Three days has passed since their kiss in his driveway and still she couldn't stop thinking about it. She was getting to him, she could tell. At this rate, she'd break down his defenses in no time. Then what would happen? She could hardly wait to find out.

She passed Ward's cubicle on the way to hers. Her *own* cubicle, she reminded herself. A ridiculously small thing, but the space symbolized her recent success...and she loved it!

"Morning, Ward," she said, peering over the wall.

"Good segment."

"Thanks." Her impossibly huge smile grew.

Sitting at her desk, she automatically pressed a button on her phone. Immediately, KPKD's current broadcast played through the speaker. She kept one ear tuned to the broadcast while she booted up her computer. Reading viewer e-mails after her report was the highlight of her day.

As she worked, her Mail Received icon flashed every few minutes. Carolina skimmed the incoming letters. She'd read them more thoroughly later. She was on the seventh one when something on the newscast caught her off guard. Turning away from her computer screen, she listened more intently.

"What the...?" Her blood went cold, then hot. Leaping from her chair, she marched into Ward's cubicle. "You liar!"

His eyebrows came together in a frown.

Carolina was instantly aware she shouldn't take such a severe tone with her boss.

She changed her approach. "You promised."

"Promised what?" he said sternly.

"The story on Neil—Sheriff Lovitt," she amended, realizing her mistake. "Leonard's reading it now." Poor Neil. He'd be crushed. Disappointed. Angry. And he'd think she was responsible.

"I made no such promise."

"Yes, you did. I'm doing the series on the illegal min—"

He didn't let her finish. "I agreed to put you in charge of the illegal mining story, but I never agreed not to run the story on Sheriff Lovitt."

Pleading with Ward was pointless. Leonard had already read the story. The damage was done.

"There's nothing more to discuss." Ward added insult to injury by turning his back to her.

Carolina reined in her emotions. Letting loose, blurting out what she really thought would get her fired. While she might feel vindicated, the fact was she could get to the bottom of what was going on with Ward and be of more help to Neil if she stayed.

"Why?" she asked. "Can you at least tell me that?"

"It's relevant news and, as you well know, we're attempting to raise the level of our newscasts."

"Bullshit," she muttered under her breath.

His eyes narrowed. "I beg your pardon?"

So much for reining in her emotions.

"Nothing." She spun on her heels and returned to her cubicle. Ward had been unpredictable lately. Dealing with him was a wasted effort.

At her desk, she opened a drawer and grabbed a tissue from a box she kept there, allowing herself a few quiet tears. A popular country-and-western song played through the speaker on her phone. The lyrics barely registered with Carolina. All that mattered to her was that the horrible newscast had ended.

Would Ward repeat it during the afternoon segment? Please, God, no.

She considered phoning Neil. If he hadn't heard the newscast, surely someone else had alerted him. What could she tell him other than that she wasn't the one behind the story? No, better to wait and contact him when she had more information.

Lately, the station owners had been pressuring all the department heads to step up their efforts to expand their listening audience. Ward could be under the gun himself, which would explain why he'd changed his mind about doing the story on Neil.

What she really needed to do was start work on her report for tomorrow. The draft was due on Ward's desk by one today. But try as she might, she couldn't focus. Neil totally consumed her thoughts.

Wait a minute!

What if she made him and the good job his department

was doing with the illegal mining investigation the focus of her report?

Yes! It wasn't much, but any positive media exposure would help offset the bad.

She returned to her computer, intending to exit out of her e-mail program. Instead, she opened the next message by mistake and automatically skimmed it.

The e-mail contained a single line and wasn't signed. With each word she read, blood drained from her face.

Stop your reports on the illegal mining or you and your family will be sorry.

Her phone rang. The shrill buzzing caused her to jerk reflexively. Without thinking, she reached for the receiver. Heart hammering, her eyes still riveted to the computer screen, she placed the phone to her ear and muttered weakly, "Hello."

A crackling pause ensued, then a sharp click as her caller disconnected.

Chapter Eleven

Neil flew past the receptionist's desk at KPKD without stopping. "Where's Carolina Sweetwater?"

"Conference room. Second door on your right."

He couldn't remember thirty feet ever taking so long to cover. The doorknob stuck and he nearly yanked it off in his haste to open the door.

Carolina sat at the long table, a man Neil assumed to be her boss beside her. She looked small, shaken and pale. Relief washed over him only to collide head-on with anger. She didn't rattle easily. Whoever had done this to her, put that stricken expression on her face, would pay. He'd see to it.

"You're here." She pushed away from the table.

He was on duty, responding to an emergency, and someone else was in the room with them. Neil didn't care. He went to her and took her trembling body in his arms.

"Are you all right?"

"I'm fine."

He needed to know for certain and touched her cheek with one hand. Her skin was cool. Everything about her was cool. And vulnerable.

He vowed again to find the bastards responsible.

"I'm sorry to bother you," she said, leaning her face into his hand.

"I'm glad you called." He released her. Reluctantly. "Are the police still here?"

"They left about ten minutes ago," her boss answered.

Neil cursed the long drive. He'd been thirty miles outside of town at the deserted Remington place when Carolina had called, her voice breathless and sounding on the verge of tears. He'd instructed her to hang up immediately and dial 911. The homeless individuals reportedly holed up in the dilapidated barn could wait. Carolina had been threatened.

The past rushed up to meet the present. The situations weren't the same but his emotions were, especially the ones that left him angry and feeling helpless. He'd failed to protect Carolina, just like he'd failed Lynne.

"Did the officer give you his name?"

"*She* left this card," her boss said, and stood.

Neil accepted the card and read the officer's name and badge number. He'd crossed paths with the woman before and knew her to be competent and thorough. That much was good.

"Thank you." He handed the card back to Carolina's boss.

"Do you need a copy?" he asked.

"No."

The atmosphere in the room suddenly became awkward. "I'll get back to work." Carolina's boss patted her arm. "Take tomorrow off, why don't you."

"I'll be fine."

"Really. In fact, take the rest of the week off."

Neil sensed her stiffen.

"You're removing me from the illegal mining story?" Her voice hitched.

"Under the circumstances, I think it would be wise."

"No, Ward. Please."

"You were threatened, Carolina."

"It was an e-mail. People in the media get hate e-mails all the time."

"We'll talk later, when you're not upset." He turned and left.

Neil couldn't say he liked her boss, especially after this morning's news bite on him. But the man was being smart. Carolina needed to be removed from the story for her own safety.

"I suppose you agree with him." She was doing her best to appear tough.

Neil didn't buy her act. "Come on. I'll drive you home."

"I can drive myself."

"Not while I'm here."

She stuck out her lower lip, reminding him of Zoey. He could see why they got along so well. Both were determined to test his patience on a daily basis.

"I'm driving you home. If you refuse, I'll cuff you and take you against your will."

"Why, Sheriff Lovitt," she said with exaggerated silkiness, "I had no clue you were so kinky."

"There's a lot you don't know about me."

That shut her up, and she went willingly with him.

While Carolina gathered her things from her cubicle, he waited in the reception area and called the Payson PD, leaving a message for the officer who'd been at the station. He ignored the receptionist, whose eyes bored into the back of his head. Let her, Carolina's boss and anyone else at the station think what they did about him. Neil had nothing to be ashamed of.

The thought stopped him in his tracks.

He'd been living with guilt and shame for four years. When had he stopped agreeing with the negative things people said about him?

The click of Carolina's heels on the tile floor alerted him

to her approach. It was obvious from the fake smile she wore that some of her bravado had left her. Taking her hand in his, he escorted her outside. He'd rather do a whole lot more. Hold her, shelter her, tuck her away in a safe corner and put her under constant guard. Anything to protect her from harm.

"I'm parked over here." At the cruiser, he opened the passenger-side door. She made a face.

"You haven't been in an official vehicle before?"

"Not in the front seat. Once or twice in the back." One corner of her mouth tipped up, and she was suddenly her old self again, if only for a moment.

It required every bit of his professional training not to grab her and bring his mouth crashing down on hers.

The ride to Bear Creek Ranch took about twenty minutes. They didn't say much during the drive. For his part, Neil was saving up until they reached her cabin, where she'd be trapped and have no avenue of escape except running. And he'd bet, in those shoes, he'd catch her in two seconds flat. When he did, he'd give her a big piece of his mind.

Pulling up in front of her gate, he helped her out of the cruiser.

"Would you like to come in for a minute," she asked with the tiniest trace of insecurity.

Just like that, all Neil's intentions went out the window.

"Yeah, sure." Just a warning, he decided, no lecture.

One step inside the cabin, she turned to face him. Two steps, she was in his arms again, all soft curves, sweet-smelling skin and needing comfort. Three steps, their jackets were off and his mouth was where he'd wanted it to be since he walked into the conference room. On hers. Taking, giving, demanding, relenting.

Good God, the relenting was insane. Without even trying, she caused him to lose control over and over again.

"I was so scared for you," he said between ragged breaths.

"I broke every traffic law getting to the station after you called."

"I'm glad you did." She arched into him, soft moans escaping her. "I wasn't sure you cared."

He abruptly stopped and pushed her away from him. "I more than care, Carolina. You matter to me. A lot." The vehemence of his admission took him aback.

It did Carolina, too, gauging by the flash in her eyes. He thought he might have gone too far, said too much. Scared her off.

She looped one arm around his neck. With her other hand, she lightly stroked the bristles of his five-o'clock shadow. "Don't talk like that, Sheriff Lovitt, unless you intend to back up your words with action."

Okay, he hadn't scared her off.

"You sure?" Talking wasn't easy, not with his chest pounding and pulse racing. "I won't stop once I get started." He cupped her bottom, lifted her flush against him so she would know exactly what she was getting into with him.

She shifted so that his erection fit more snugly into the junction of her legs. Yeah, she knew.

"For the record," she murmured, "you matter a lot to me, too."

This was insane. He should stop. Once they crossed the line, there was no going back.

Her fingertips dug into his muscles of his shoulders. "Did you bring protection?"

A jolt of sexual energy ripped through him. The hell with going back. There was only ahead.

"I'm an officer of the law." He lowered his mouth, pressed his lips to the shallow dip at the base of her neck and tasted her skin. "It's my sworn duty to protect."

"And you're good at your job." She smiled coyly.

"I haven't carried a condom in my wallet since Lynne and

I dated." He skimmed his hand up her back, kneading the pliant flesh his fingers encountered. "Until recently." Did she understand the meaning of what he'd just said?

"When did you start?"

"The night I dropped you off here." When they'd first kissed. "It was wrong and stupid and—"

"I went out and bought a box the next day. Just in case."

"You did?"

She nibbled at his bottom lip, teased it with her tongue. "A girl can always hope."

The meaning of her words wasn't lost on him, either.

"I guess we're good to go." He grinned.

"All night long."

"I have to pick up Zoey later."

"Then all afternoon."

He could do all afternoon, assuming no calls came in. "There's something else I should tell you." His hand slipped inside her blouse. Her skin was like silk, smooth, warm and inviting. "Along with protecting you, it's also my sworn duty to serve." His fingers dipped into the waistband of her skirt, fumbled for her zipper. "I consider it the most important part of my job."

She shivered and cuddled closer. "Who am I to interfere with your sworn duty? Especially the most important part."

A minute later, she was naked, and he was thanking God the last shred of his good sense had abandoned him.

CAROLINA WOULD HAVE TAKEN Neil to her bedroom, but the couch was closer. She sank into the plush cushions, pulling him down with her. There was something incredibly erotic about her being utterly naked and him being fully clothed—in his uniform, no less. Her bare calf rubbed against his khaki pant leg. The tips of her breasts skimmed the front of his shirt and the pockets with their mother-of-pearl snaps. The cool metal of his belt buckle nestled in the warm curve of her belly.

Erotic, indeed.

Also frustrating. She wanted him naked, too.

"Take this off." She removed his cowboy hat and flung it... somewhere. "And this."

When she tried to strip him of his shirt, he eased out of her reach. "Not yet." He moved down the length of her body, leaving a trail of goose bumps in his wake. "Not until I'm done."

"With what?"

"You." He plumped her breast with his hand, then took her beaded nipple in his mouth.

She stopped breathing. Stopped thinking. Stopped trying to put into words what she felt and just let myriad pleasurable sensations crash over her one by one.

His talent was unequaled, she thought distractedly as he kissed his way to her other breast. They should erect a shrine in his honor. No, no, she amended as his tongue circled and teased and flicked over profoundly sensitive regions that had lain dormant much too long. She wanted to keep his skills her own little secret.

He nudged her legs apart, causing her to gasp. She'd been so occupied with losing herself in the sensual delights of his touch that she'd failed to notice he'd once again changed positions, sliding lower on her body and stopping only when his mouth was level with her lower belly.

She watched him through half-closed eyes, her anticipation building as he stroked and caressed her most intimate spots. Nothing had ever aroused her more.

He made her wait, damn him, driving her crazy with feather-light touches. When his mouth finally descended on her, she was ready to fly apart. He made her wait for that, too, expertly keeping her poised on the precipice for...oh, my!

Her climax was sudden and earth-shattering and seemingly endless. Maybe she just didn't want it to end. Who would? Time, perhaps, to reconsider that shrine.

"What did you say?" he murmured, wearing an infuriating and well-deserved grin.

"Nothing." She moved languorously.

"Yes, you did. Something about a shrine."

Her cheeks instantly heated. Make that overheated. She was already flushed from head to toe.

"I said that was fine."

"It was more than fine." He got up and started undressing.

"Okay. On a scale of one to ten, it was a—"

Carolina's mind went blank, wiped clean by the sight of Neil shirtless. When his pants and briefs followed, her system poised on the verge of shutdown. It wasn't merely a five-year abstinence that made Carolina appreciate Neil's honed physique and impressive arousal. The man was Greek-statue worthy.

He dug the condom out of his wallet before tossing his pants aside.

"I'll take that." She held out her hand.

His grin went from sexy to dangerous in the span of a heartbeat. "You sure?"

"Very."

He dropped the condom into her open palm. She promptly set it on the end table.

"I thought—"

"All in good time," she promised before he could say more. Taking his hand, she guided him down beside her and welcomed him with a kiss that went from sweet to demanding in three seconds flat. She heightened their shared excitement by reaching between them to cup and stroke and fondle every inch of him.

When he moved over her, she pushed him back. "Not yet."

He grunted in protest but relented and let her have her way with him. She left the very intense pleasure of his mouth to explore other parts of his body. Neck. Chest. Abdomen. Thighs.

"Carolina." Her name was a hoarse whisper that seemed to tear from his lips.

She replied by taking him fully into her hands, then into her mouth.

He hung on for another thirty seconds before demanding, "Put the damn condom on."

"Soon." He'd made her wait, and turnabout was fair play.

Neil, however, wasn't patient and, in her opinion, a spoilsport. Without warning, he hoisted her up onto the couch and into his lap so that she straddled him, one leg on each side. He reached for the condom. She beat him to it, ripping it open with a flourish.

Then, thank heaven, he was inside her, fulfilling every single one of the fantasies she'd indulged in since the day of her sister's wedding. And she had a very vivid imagination.

Neil didn't talk, not that she expected he would. He let his body speak for him, but Carolina couldn't resist murmuring into his ear about how good he was making her feel.

Neil cupped her bottom, thrusting harder and deeper. She adjusted to the new rhythm, adding a little of her own. He swore, which Carolina took as an indication he liked her innovativeness, then gave himself over to a violent shudder.

She cradled his head and held it to her breasts. Kissing the top of his hair, now damp with sweat, she rode the remainder of his release with him, rocking them both until he was spent at last.

When his ragged breathing slowed, he sweetly nuzzled the underside of her breast, repeating her name. A rush of tender emotions filled Carolina, and her throat unexpectedly closed. The great sex hadn't surprised her. Considering the sparks that had flared between them, it was a given. What had taken her by storm was the intensity and depth of her feelings for him.

Then it hit her. She didn't just like Neil, wasn't simply attracted to him. She was falling for him. Completely.

What now?

Would he regret what they'd done? She sure as heck didn't. Would he tell her that, despite everything, they weren't getting involved because of his stupid hang-ups about danger and all the other BS he'd handed her? If so, she had the perfect answer.

Rather than panic and drive herself batty by attempting to analyze what was going on with her and Neil and where it might lead, she relaxed. Or tried to. Fear that they would lapse into an awkward moment kept her from enjoying herself.

Then Neil hugged her. His arms came up, circled her and pulled her close so that her breasts lay flat against his chest and his face fit perfectly into the side of her neck. She couldn't help but respond. Slowly, bit by bit, her limbs turned to liquid and her heart to mush.

"I'd like to do this again," he mumbled. "Soon."

"Right away soon?" She thought she detected a slight stirring beneath her, and he *had* mentioned all afternoon.

"I wish." He gave a robust groan when the radio attached to his shirt crackled and a disembodied female voice spewed codes that made no sense to Carolina. "I have to return to the station."

"Are you still on duty?" She should have realized that.

"Technically, yes."

The thought made her feel exquisitely naughty.

"Drats." She rose from the couch to get dressed. Sort of. She stopped at panties and her blouse, which she only partially buttoned. He seemed to like ogling her cleavage and legs, so she indulged him.

At the door, he swooped her into his arms for a goodbye kiss. Then two, then three. They were starting to feel like hello kisses when he set her aside.

"I have to go."

"Call me?" Afraid she sounded a bit anxious, she affected a lighter tone. "If you want."

"You know I want." His hand pressed into the small of her back.

That was better.

"I didn't plan this," he said.

"Me neither." She snuggled deeper into his embrace. "But I'm glad it happened." A profound pause followed.

Like that, the doubts Carolina had previously dismissed returned to plague her.

"Just in case you don't know it," she said breezily, "this is the part where you jump in and enthusiastically agree with me."

"I'm glad. Believe me." He spoke with such conviction she couldn't help but be relieved. "But I'm also concerned."

"About where this is going?"

"That, too."

"Don't ruin the mood, Neil, by bringing up work and the mine and danger."

"I worry about you."

Because he cared. Hadn't he told her as much? Twice, if she remembered correctly. "I worry about you, too. You're far more likely to land in trouble or get hurt than me."

The change in his expression was instantaneous.

"Let me guess," she said. "Lynne told you the same thing."

"Let's talk about this later. I really need to stop by the station, then pick up Zoey."

She bristled—she couldn't help it. His excuse was a valid one but smacked of a brush-off.

"All right." Feeling suddenly vulnerable, she fastened the rest of the buttons on her blouse. The shield was a flimsy one at best and no defense against Neil.

To prove it, he swooped her up into an embrace, slipped his hand inside her blouse and fondled her breast as if to say the hell with her and stake his claim. A Neanderthal and chauvinistic move if ever Carolina saw one.

That didn't stop her from loving it.

"I'll call you," he said determinedly, his fingers making all sorts of unspoken promises.

If not for the very tenuous thread of pride she clung to, she might have dissolved into a puddle.

"I have to go out and won't be home later."

"I'll track you down."

She believed him, and the lovely little tingle in her middle bloomed into a full-fledged fluttering. This silly, girly-girl stuff had to stop. It was so not like her.

He bent his head for another goodbye kiss. Carolina knew it would truly be the last when his radio went off again and she heard the female voice distinctly say, "Bear Creek Ranch." She thrust away from Neil. "What's going on?"

He didn't answer her question. Pressing a button on his radio, he spoke into it. "On my way."

"Neil."

"Later." He was out the door in a flash.

"I'm one of the owners." She chased after him, mindless of the cool temperature and that she was only half-dressed. "I have a right to know."

"The mining site's been broken into, and the equipment belonging to the Arizona Geological Society vandalized." Neil rounded the cruiser and yanked open the driver's-side door.

Carolina spent exactly two seconds deliberating what to do. "I'll meet you there. I just have to get dressed."

"No!" He stood with one hand on the open cruiser door. The other, balled into a fist, rested on the roof. "Stay put. You got it? Don't you set foot within a mile of that mine until I give you the all clear." He didn't wait for her to reply. Jumping into the cruiser, he sped off, leaving a plume of dust behind.

Stay put? Not on her life.

No sooner was she inside than she got on the phone and called Jake.

Chapter Twelve

"Carolina! Hey, where you off to?"

"The sub shop." She waited for Adrian, the station's techie, to catch up with her. "Want me to grab you something?"

"Mind if I go with you?"

"Not at all."

She felt no discomfort issuing the invitation. He hadn't asked her out again or shown any interest in her for weeks. Come to think of it, no man had. Was she giving off some sort of unconscious vibes since... She'd started to think *hooking up with Neil,* but that wasn't exactly right.

He hadn't called her since their afternoon together three days ago, as he said he would. Probably because she'd shown up at the mining site that night with Jake and her sister Rachel. They weren't allowed near the tunnel, and though Neil spoke with them, it was in an official capacity only.

Hard to imagine he'd been in her arms a mere hour earlier.

His eyes, however, had spoken volumes. They let her know he wasn't happy she'd defied his instructions to remain home.

And he hadn't called since.

It was obvious he didn't want her interfering with the investigation, didn't want her reporting on it—too late for that—and didn't want her leaving her cabin.

Well, forget it. Listeners were eating up her reports, and the station's ratings had escalated through the roof. The owners were pleased, giving her a special acknowledgment at the last staff meeting, and insisted she continue until further notice. On top of that, Jake's administrative assistant had reported reservations at the ranch were exceeding projections. The family couldn't be happier.

If only Ward were as pleased with her. Since the phone call and the threatening e-mail, he'd been acting even more out of sorts.

What was it with her and men lately?

Adrian appeared to be the exception. He increased his pace to match hers and headed toward the door.

"Let me get that." He rushed to open it for her.

"Thank you." She refrained from staring openmouthed. Adrian was cute and charming in a nerdy kind of way. Gentlemanly manners weren't his style.

At the curb, he placed a hand on her arm and halted her when she would have crossed the street.

"Jeez, Adrian, what's up with you?"

"Nothing."

"Seriously. You're no Boy Scout, and I'm no old lady."

"A car was coming."

"The light was red."

"The driver might have run the light. You can't be too careful."

She laughed. "Quit joking, and tell me what's going on."

He was too ingenuous to hide his guilt. "Ward asked me to watch out for you."

"Ward?" She was dumbfounded.

"He's worried about you."

"Oh, pull-eeze." She looked around, wondering for half a second if there were any hidden cameras in the area. "Ward's not exactly a role model for a concerned boss."

"You're wrong. He was really upset when you got that e-mail."

"He wasn't the only one."

Carolina still couldn't open an e-mail from a sender she didn't recognize without enduring a bout of nervous anxiety. She hadn't talked about it with Neil yet, but there had to be a connection between his phone calls and hers.

"He didn't think you should go to the sub shop alone," Adrian said.

"What?" Her boss was totally flipping out. What could happen to her in the middle of the day, in the middle of town and with people everywhere?

Then she remembered. Neil's wife, Lynne, had died under just such circumstances.

Carolina immediately shook off the thought. That was New York. Not Payson.

"Whatever the reason," she said to Adrian, "I'm glad you came along. I like the company."

"Good report this morning. I heard the guys from the Arizona Geological Society might have seen a vehicle leaving the scene."

"A white Ford Suburban. They passed it on their way back to the mine. Didn't catch the license plate, unfortunately."

"Must be a hundred white Ford Suburbans in Gila County."

"Exactly. And this one's probably stolen anyway."

They reached the sub shop counter and placed their orders.

"What about gold? Did the investigators find any?"

Adrian was sure asking a lot of questions. Up until now, he hadn't been all that interested in her stories on the illegal mining.

"They've given us a preliminary report." She was purposely evasive. The family had agreed to wait to announce the investigation results until they received the final report and decided what to do.

They chatted about work until a harried clerk called out, "Number seventy-two."

Carolina and Adrian retrieved their sandwiches.

"You want to eat here?" he asked.

"Can't. I have to finish up my draft on tomorrow's report so Ward can okay it."

Adrian took her arm again at the corner and held it while they crossed the street. She didn't know whether to be amused, flattered or annoyed.

"What are you reporting on next?" he asked.

"I'm interviewing the team from the Arizona Geological Society. Getting a follow-up from them on the vandalism." Jake had spent half of yesterday afternoon on the phone with the ranch's insurance company, making sure the team's equipment would be paid for. "I wish I had something new to report." She might if Neil ever called.

"Have you been out to the mining site lately?"

"Not since the night of the vandalism. We're not allowed. The police have it cordoned off again."

"Too bad you couldn't do a live broadcast from there."

Carolina's feet came to a grinding halt. "What a great idea, Adrian! You're a genius."

He grinned sheepishly. "No, I'm not."

"Seriously. That's a fantastic idea." She was already picturing the live broadcast in her head. "I can't believe I didn't think of it."

"I mean, it's not really my idea. Ward was talking about a live broadcast during your report this morning."

"He was? How come he didn't mention it to me?"

Was he attempting to keep her out of harm's way again? Or were he and Neil in cahoots?

"I'm going to hit Ward up the second we get back. Suggest

we include the interview with the team from the geological society."

"What about Sheriff Lovitt?"

"What about him?

"Won't he object?"

Did everyone at the station know about her and Neil?

"He may." That was an understatement. Neil would blow his top and get all sheriffy on her. "I can deal with him."

Could she?

Carolina and Adrian parted ways at the receptionist's desk.

"Good luck," he told her.

"Thanks." She'd need her fair share to pull this off.

THERE HAD BEEN a total of seven articles to date about Neil in the Payson paper and sixteen letters to the editor, a couple in support but mostly not. He sat at his desk, reading the latest article when he should be tackling the mountain of reports awaiting review. Nothing new had been printed in the paper, just the same old stuff about Lynne and the IA investigation. So as not to show bias, the paper had also inserted a paragraph—a *tiny* paragraph—about his exemplary service to the county since coming to Payson.

If he were a regular subscriber, he'd be getting pretty tired of reading about Neil Lovitt by now.

He set his half-eaten lunch aside and flipped to the editorial page. Only two of the letters were about him today, and of those, just one appeared negative. A fifty/fifty ratio. The percentages were getting better. He had Carolina to thank for that, at least in part. Her positively slanted reports on his investigation of the illegal mining operation had cast him in a good light.

His own efforts also helped. Before Lynne's death, Neil had been a good cop and a good investigating officer. He was glad to discover he hadn't lost his skill…or his enthusiasm for the work.

More than ever, he remained convinced someone with an ulterior motive had it in for him, though he still didn't know who or why. If they could get even one small break on the case, chances were folks—and the newspaper—would forget all about his past.

A copy of the geological society's preliminary report had been faxed over to him from Bear Creek Ranch that afternoon. The results weren't what he'd expected, and he'd be interested in learning what the family's plans were.

Not that Carolina would tell him. They hadn't spoken since he left her cabin after making love with her. His fault. He should have called her. But everything had become so complicated so quickly.

She must hate him.

He really needed to man up and call her.

He laid down the newspaper and reached for the phone. Face-to-face would be better, but he had an open house at Zoey's school tonight and didn't want to wait another day before talking to Carolina. His hand was just lifting the receiver when Otis strolled into his office.

"Hey! What are you doing here?" Neil returned the phone to its cradle, fighting a mixture of disappointment and relief.

"I escaped Patty's clutches."

"Good for you."

"Actually, she has a meeting over at the Historical Society and dropped me off out front." The sheriff sat down in the visitor chair. "She figured I couldn't get into too much trouble in an hour."

"She doesn't know you well, does she?"

Otis's loud laugh filled the room. "If I'm lucky, their speaker will run over, and I'll have an extra hour to chew the fat with you. Could happen. He's the assistant curator from the museum."

"Really?" Neil had been in contact with Mr. Dunstan several times over the past week.

"He's talking to Patty's group about the early mining that went on here. Everyone's interested, naturally, what with the illegal digging at Bear Creek Ranch. And not just locally. We've had a flood of new tourists lately."

Neil knew that from the increase in traffic citations.

"Well, if anything, it's good for the economy. Who said crime doesn't pay?" Otis laughed again and rocked back in his chair. He studied Neil at length. "You look good behind that desk."

The change in their usual positions hadn't been lost on Neil. He'd experienced a fleeting moment of discomfort when Otis had first entered the room.

"The chair's a little roomy. Might be a bit more than I'm capable of filling."

"Don't underestimate yourself, Neil. You're doing a bang-up job."

"I'm not sure about that. And besides, I won't be sitting here much longer."

"Who knows? I have to retire eventually." Otis's features fell slightly. "One thing this heart attack has taught me, I won't be around forever."

"You have a lot of years left."

"I may not want to spend all of them in that chair. I've shortchanged Patty something awful during our marriage. She's a good woman, a good wife, and deserves more than I've given her."

"She loves you, Otis."

"Don't know why." He shook off his display of emotion with a grunt.

Neil tapped the folded newspaper beside his desk blotter. "Have you read the latest?"

"Ridiculous drivel."

Neil took that as a no.

"What you need to do is find out who the hell's behind the illegal mining."

"I was thinking the same thing myself right before you walked in."

"Any progress?"

For reasons he couldn't explain, Neil hesitated telling Otis about the preliminary report from the geological society. Not that he didn't trust Otis, but the fewer people who knew about the team's findings, the better.

"Not much," he told Otis. "The wheels are moving slow."

"Good! Maybe we can draw this out a little longer, just until the economy in this town turns all the way around."

"Yeah," Neil said pensively.

Without meaning to, Otis may have hit on something. Everyone assumed the motive behind the illegal mining was to extract gold for resale on the black market. What if it wasn't? What if the purpose was to generate interest and bring tourists to Payson? Who would have the most to gain in that scenario?

The first names that came to mind were the owners of Bear Creek Ranch. The place where the illegal mining had occurred.

Neil set that thought aside and, for the next fifteen minutes, he and Otis discussed the department and how Neil was progressing with the deputies.

"Not good, but better," he said. "Like me, they're laying low, waiting for you to return."

"You can add Patty to that list. She's plumb tired of having me constantly underfoot."

"R.J. might be responsible for bringing the men in line. He's been a good supporter."

"He's just a good man all-around."

"You got that right."

Otis braced his hands on the arms of the visitor chair and hoisted himself out of his seat. "I'd better get a move on. Let you get back to your lunch."

"I'm glad you stopped by."

"Me, too." He surprised Neil by reaching across the desk and shaking his hand. "You've conducted yourself well during this mess and deserve to be congratulated. Makes me glad I recommended you to the county commissioner."

"Thank you, sir." The compliment touched Neil.

After Otis ambled out of the office, Neil picked up the remaining half of his sandwich and the newspaper, flipping to the editorial page. He ate on automatic pilot, his attention completely focused on the more positive letter to the editor.

At the last paragraph, he paused then reread it. The letter writer mentioned a number of Neil's accomplishments during his year-and-a-half as deputy sheriff, including the time he'd administered CPR to a heart attack victim living in Bliss Canyon. If not for his action, the elderly woman might have died.

Neil hadn't considered himself a hero, he'd simply been doing his duty. There'd been very little notice of the incident after it happened except for a brief mention in the newspaper that excluded Neil's role. He'd liked it that way, having no wish to draw attention to himself.

Which told him the person who wrote this letter either had amazing resources or was there the night he'd responded to the call. That limited the possibilities to someone on the hospital staff or the other two deputies on duty that night, Hank and R.J.

If Neil had to guess the author of the anonymous letter,

he'd pick R.J. Neil didn't know whether to thank his deputy or chew him out.

Reading the letter made him realize not everything about the job of acting sheriff was bad.

His intercom abruptly buzzed, shaking him from his thoughts. "Yes."

"Sorry to bother you, Neil." Mary Twohorses was on the line. "Can I speak to Otis?"

"He left a few minutes ago."

"Oh. I must have missed him."

"Can I help you with something?"

"No, it's all right. I have Ward Preston from KPKD holding. I'll tell him Otis left already."

Neil hung up, unable to dismiss the nagging feeling that had come from nowhere. Why would Carolina's boss be calling Otis? And how did he even know that Otis was at the station? Neil tried to focus on the pile of reports but his mind kept returning to Otis and Carolina's boss and any possible connection. Not that the two men couldn't be friends, but as far as Neil knew, they never had been.

A few minutes later his intercom buzzed again.

"Sorry, Neil," Mary said again. "But a call just came in, and I thought you should know about it."

"What's going on?"

"Carolina Sweetwater and a crew from the radio station have shown up at the illegal mining site. They're attempting to do a live broadcast."

Chapter Thirteen

Neil bolted from his chair and grabbed his hat off the credenza. "Call my babysitter for me and tell her I may be late. If she can't pick up Zoey from the riding stables, let me know."

"You got it!" Mary stepped back in the nick of time. Otherwise, he might have trampled her.

He took the old Jeep rather than his cruiser. The four-wheel-drive vehicle didn't disappoint him. Arriving at the mining site, he parked beside the radio station's brightly painted van and cut the ignition. R.J. and Hank were already there. From what Neil could see, they were making little headway with Carolina and her two-man crew.

The ground underneath his boots crunched as he tromped up the slope. He stopped on a level area about twenty feet away from the mine entrance and the yellow caution tape Carolina and her crew were trying to breach.

Refusing to be intimated, she stood tall and strong and fierce, a look of grim determination on her face. Her lavender skirt—*lavender,* for Pete's sake—hugged her legs, making a ridiculous contrast to the green trench coat she never seemed to be without.

Quite frankly, she took his breath away.

He should have phoned her before now. Maybe then the impact of seeing her wouldn't be having such a profound effect on him. Or maybe not. In the next instant, their gazes locked, and they engaged in a nonverbal standoff Neil doubted he'd win.

Could she and her family have staged this whole event just so she could use the reports to advance her career and the ranch could benefit from the increase in business?

No, he didn't think so. Seeing her rooted there, ready to take on the entire sheriff's department if necessary, he knew her motives were purely journalistic and nothing personal. KPKD might be a small radio station serving a small market, but Carolina brought a big market attitude to her job.

"R.J.," he called. His deputy came running, leaving Hank in charge of crowd control. "Report."

"Ms. Sweetwater insists that, as one of the property owners and a representative of the media, she has a right to be here."

"I bet she does." Neil reassessed the situation. "I'll talk to her."

"Want me to radio for backup?"

Did his deputy think he'd need it? "Hold off. See if I can't handle her myself."

R.J. nearly split a shirt seam laughing.

Neil wasn't amused. "I appreciate the vote of confidence."

"She's a corker, that one." R.J. attempted to wipe the smirk from his face with the back of his hand.

How much did his deputies know about his and Carolina's relationship? Neil didn't know or, he realized with a slight start, care. When had his feelings on that subject changed?

More importantly, why?

"Corker or not, the law is the law." Neil eyed Carolina.

As if anticipating his next move, she stood even taller, the flaps of her coat waving in the breeze.

Neil was more than ready for a showdown and did a little

posturing himself. "By the way," he said to R.J. before moving on, "thanks for writing that letter to the newspaper."

"What letter?"

"The one to the editor. It was in this afternoon's edition. Your support means a lot to me."

R.J. pushed his hat back and scratched his head. "You say it was a good letter?"

"Yeah. Real nice."

"Well, I'll be damned."

"What?"

"I didn't write that letter, Sheriff."

Neil frowned. "I thought maybe you did. It mentioned me giving CPR to that old woman in Bliss Canyon."

"Hank did it."

"What?"

"He bragged to the guys about writing a letter to the paper. We told him not to. Course, that's cuz we figured he'd take the low road." R.J.'s face broke out into a huge grin. "Guess we were wrong."

Neil gave his head a small shake. Hank wrote the letter? He gazed up the slope to where the deputy stood, his broad figure effectively blocking any entrance to the mine shaft.

There had to be a mistake. Maybe the letter was written by someone at the hospital. But how would anyone at the hospital know about the other incidents mentioned? Now that Neil thought about it, Hank had been on every one of those calls.

But the deputy didn't like Neil. Didn't respect him. He resented Neil for getting the appointment he felt had belonged to him.

"Let's get this over with," Neil said.

Still grinning, R.J. followed Neil up the hill. "This ought to be real good."

About ten feet from Carolina and her crew, Neil stopped

again and motioned with a small jerk of his head for Hank to join him. The deputy responded. Still built like the record-breaking halfback he'd been in junior college, he lumbered over, his features cross, his beefy hands knotted at his sides. "Yes, sir."

Sir? That was new.

"I'd like to encourage these fine folks to leave with as little trouble as possible," Neil said.

"Carolina won't go without a fight."

Since when did Hank refer to Carolina by her first name? Neil's hackles rose, though he refused to show it. He didn't have exclusive rights to Carolina's first name, even if he wanted them.

"Nice letter to the editor." R.J. socked Hank in the arm. "Way to go, pal."

Hank's stern features softened momentarily, then grew dark again. "I don't know what you're talking about."

"Right," R.J. scoffed.

"Shut up." Hank elbowed R.J. hard in the ribs.

Neil wasn't sure what to make of their antics. "Hank?"

"Yes, sir."

Sir again? "Did you write the letter?"

"Well…" The young deputy faltered. "Didn't seem right that folks were talking trash about you."

Neil swallowed his shock. "I appreciate it."

"I don't always agree with you, sir, but we need to stick up for our own. If we don't, who else will?"

"Call me Neil." He put out his hand.

Hank shook it. "Yes, sir. Neil."

"You two watch the mine entrance." It was time to get this job done. "I'll see if I can't defuse the situation."

"Sure you don't want me to radio for backup?" R.J. visibly held in a chuckle. Neil couldn't tell but he thought Hank might be hiding a smile, as well. So much for maintaining a position of authority.

"Get after it," he barked.

R.J. and Hank strode over to the yellow caution tape barrier and positioned themselves behind it. All eyes were on Neil as he approached the group.

"Ms. Sweetwater." He addressed her calmly and professionally. "Can I help you with something?"

"My team and I would like access to the mine for a live broadcast." She sent him an icy stare.

He didn't wilt. Ice he could handle. It was her fire that robbed him of his senses and turned him to putty in her hands.

"I'm sorry, Ms. Sweetwater," he said in his best cop voice, "but this is a crime scene, and we can't risk contamination."

"We have a right to be here."

"You can conduct your broadcast from the base of the slope but not here." He could tell from her expression she hadn't expected him to concede even that much.

"We prefer to do it from the actual crime scene." She formed her lips into a stubborn pout.

Given the chance, he'd cover her lips with his and kiss her until pouting was the furthest thing from her mind. Unfortunately, he'd have to wait for another day. Like tomorrow. When he told her in private just how idiotic her little scheme was.

"Will it make a difference? Your listeners can't see the mine. You could be broadcasting from the dining hall at Bear Creek Ranch for all they'd know."

She inhaled sharply. Neil had found her hot button. The geeky guy beside her giggled, then choked when she glared at him.

"No need for you to be insulting," she said to Neil.

"No need for you to be stupid," he fired back. "There's evidence in that mine that could lead to the identification and arrest of the criminals behind the illegal digging. I can't allow you and your crew to stomp all over it."

"We will not stomp—"

"If you don't leave now, I'll have the three of you arrested."

"Just try."

"Don't push me, Carolina." Somewhere along the way, Neil realized, the battle had become personal. "I'm not joking around."

She didn't give an inch. "I suppose that means an interview with you is out of the question."

"If that's what it takes to get you to leave, then yes."

"No, thank you." She pulled herself together. "I don't need to negotiate for an interview."

Her words were reminiscent of the ones she'd uttered during an earlier argument, only that one had been about their relationship.

Wasn't this one, too?

"My men will help you down," he said through a very tightly clenched jaw.

"We're not leaving. Not until—"

In the next instant, a gunshot rang out.

"Take cover!" Hank shouted, and dived for Carolina's two crew members, taking them both down at the same time. The trio hit with a loud, bone-crunching thud.

Neil didn't think. He grabbed Carolina and tossed her to the ground, covering her with his body. More bullets whizzed past their heads. Four, five, six. Neil could hear them pinging off the rocks just above them. The blood in his veins instantly froze, and he was thrust back in time to the deli and the day Lynne died from a stray bullet.

It took all his willpower to remain rooted in the present.

If he didn't, if he let the memories get a stranglehold on him and affect his judgment, he might not be able to keep Carolina and the others safe.

"ARE YOU ALL RIGHT?" Neil raised himself up slightly on one elbow.

Carolina lay beneath him, warm and breathing, but that was no guarantee she hadn't been hit and was slowly bleeding out.

"Yes," she squeaked.

"Don't move. You hear me? This isn't the time to argue."

"I won't."

Her face, just inches from his, was stark white, and her lips trembled. Good. For once, she'd probably behave.

"R.J.?" he called.

"Over here, Sheriff. I'm fine."

"Hank?"

"We're all okay."

That was a relief. The bullets had been close. *Very* close. They were lucky no one was shot.

Lucky, or intentional?

The gunfire had come from nearby. Just over the ridge. They should all be dead, but they weren't.

"You want me to call for that backup now?" R.J. asked from behind a boulder where he'd taken cover.

"Yes. And everybody stay down!"

Neil didn't have much hope the shooter would still be in the area when their backup arrived. And he'd bet when they located the spot the shooter had fired from, not one piece of evidence would be there. Not even a hair follicle.

If he'd had any doubts before, this afternoon had erased them. The criminals they were dealing with were professionals.

"There's a rock sticking in my back." Carolina shifted.

He pinned her with an arm across her chest. "I don't care if it's sticking in your...never mind. Don't move until I give you the go-ahead."

"Neil?" she whispered.

"Yes."

"That was scary."

His heart constricted. "I know, sweetheart." He'd been scared, too. Out of his mind. Every time he blinked, he saw the image of Lynne's blood splattered all over the side of the building. "But he's gone now, and you're okay."

"You sure he's gone?"

"Not so sure that I'm going to let you up before our backup arrives." He could hear R.J. radioing in for assistance and Hank attempting to calm the two crew members.

"Adrian, Miguel," Carolina called out. "Are you all right?"

"I'm fine. Miguel's having a meltdown."

"So what if I am? We almost died."

"Yeah, but we'll be front-page news," Adrian answered. "Think of the publicity."

"That's the spirit," Carolina answered.

"Keep quiet," Neil ordered. "We don't know if the shooter is still out there and what he'll do."

All was silent for several minutes. Neil tried to twist the upper half of his body around so he could scan the area.

"Thank you." Carolina's warm breath caressed his cheek, distracting him.

"For what?"

"Saving me." She lifted her head and kissed him. Soft, sweet and tender.

Because he could have lost her today, because he'd wanted to kiss her so badly earlier and couldn't, because everything he'd worried would happen to her *had* happened, he kissed her back, and to hell with what his deputies and her crew thought.

She clung to him as if this was their last moment together. Maybe it should be. Once again, his job had put a person he cared about in danger.

Unable to continue gazing into her liquid hazel eyes, he averted his head. "Your coat's dirty."

She seemed unaware of his distress. "A small price to pay."

"Hey, Sheriff," R.J. called. "I think I can make it to the mine shaft. You want me to try? I might be able to see the road. That shooter didn't walk here."

"Stay low."

"Will do."

Neil listened to the sound of his deputy crawling across the ground, listened harder for any movement in the distance.

"What do you see?"

"Nothing," R.J. responded. "Not even a dust cloud. I'm thinking he's clean gone." A few minutes later, he announced, "Here comes our backup."

Neil felt Carolina relax. He wished he could do the same. Whoever had shot at them was still out there and would likely try again. Only next time, the shots might not be warning ones fired over their heads.

Fifteen minutes later, Carolina's crew was safely ensconced in the rear seat of a Payson Police Department cruiser and seemed quite content to wait there.

Carolina wasn't patient. She was supposed to be sitting in the front seat but kept hopping out, only to be firmly escorted back. If she'd had her way, she and her crew would be doing the live broadcast that had brought them to the illegal mining site in the first place. When she'd called her boss, however, he had demonstrated good judgment and vetoed the idea.

"Hi, Carmen." Neil had phoned his babysitter to inform

her that he'd be delayed. "I know it's a lot to ask, but can you pick Zoey up at the stables?"

"No problem, Sheriff."

Sheriff. He involuntarily tensed. If he weren't acting sheriff, none of this would have happened. Carolina wouldn't have almost died.

"Thanks. I'll pay you double."

"Well, I won't refuse," Carmen said. "Tuition for next semester's coming up, and I can use the money."

"See you later, then." Neil disconnected. He was more than happy to pay Carmen extra for her services. An idea had started forming in the back of his mind, and if everything came together, he might not need his babysitter's services anymore. He wanted to compensate her as much as possible before then.

"You ready to head back to the station?" a detective from the Payson Police Department asked Neil. The two agencies continued to work closely together on the illegal mining investigation. Neil would be required to give them a report along with one for the sheriff's department.

"Let's go." He almost made it back to his cruiser.

"Neil?" Carolina materialized beside him.

How did she get away from the cruiser? He glanced around, trying to see who wasn't doing their job.

"You need to get back." He reached for her arm.

"What's going to happen?" The tough exterior she presented to everyone else cracked, revealing a rarely seen vulnerable side.

"You'll be taken to the Payson police station to give a statement."

"Not tonight. I mean, with us."

"I'll call you."

"Like you did the last time?"

He deserved that.

"How about you come over—" she moved to stand near him "—and we talk in person?"

The gesture was subtle but he understood it. She was giving him the opportunity to touch her, possibly hug or hold her, offer the reassurance she needed.

Too bad he couldn't do it.

"That's a good idea. Are you free tomorrow after lunch?"

"I'll make sure I am." She reached for his hand. "I'm looking forward to it."

She wouldn't be if she had any idea what he planned to say.

Chapter Fourteen

"I'm fine," Carolina insisted.

"You sure, sweetie?"

"Absolutely." Her sisters, Rachel, Corrine and Vi, hovered around her like a trio of mothers leaving their children at preschool for the first time.

The idea of them lunching together in the ranch's dining hall had appealed to Carolina, but as it turned out, the noise and commotion of a hundred other diners simultaneously eating their meals grated on her nerves. Every time someone dropped a plate or scraped a chair across the floor, she jumped.

All in all, she'd rather be at work. Her boss, however, had insisted she stay home the rest of the week. As a result, she was fighting off a chronic case of anxiety as well as her sisters' irritating yet well-intentioned coddling.

She was also worried about her job. Ward probably would take her off the mining story. He'd come close after she'd received the threatening e-mail. He might even decide to let her go altogether. After yesterday, she'd become something of a liability to the station.

"You could have been killed," Vi repeated her earlier scolding in proper older-sister fashion. "What in the world were you doing out there to begin with?"

"My job." Carolina didn't let her sister's sharp tone annoy her. Vi always came on strong.

Besides, the previous evening and night had been wretched for Carolina. She was usually one to rebound quickly. Being used as a moving target by some sicko creep had been more than even she could handle.

She really wished Neil had accompanied her when she'd given her statement. Without his comfort and protection, the seriousness of her close call had hit her hard. Returning to a dark, empty cabin after a grueling interview at the police station had driven the point home.

Her cabin had always been her sanctuary. A safe and secure haven she could retreat to with no fears. Instead, she'd spent a sleepless night ducking around corners and avoiding windows, the ping of ricocheting bullets resounding in her ears. Thank goodness Rachel had stayed with her. About three in the morning, Carolina had finally drifted off into a restless sleep, only to wake up shortly after dawn, more exhausted than when she'd gone to bed.

Neil was right. She'd been in far more danger than she realized and should have listened to him. When she saw him—any minute now—she'd tell him that and a whole lot more.

Like how crazy she was about him and how there weren't any obstacles they couldn't overcome together.

"You have to eat," Rachel chided.

"I am."

"Not enough. You haven't had anything substantial since lunch yesterday."

It was true. Carolina had missed dinner because of being at the police station, and breakfast, too. Much as she'd tried, the idea of putting even one bite of toast in her mouth had caused her stomach to roil in protest. The chicken noodle soup sitting in front of her was going down a little easier.

"See." Carolina lifted her spoon high and took another bite.

Great. While she'd been stalling, the soup had grown cold.

Would she ever be able to relax again? Not hear the bullets or relive the horror? She didn't dare tell her sisters about her anxiety. They'd insist she see a therapist when all she needed was time. And Neil. He was better than any counselor's advice could ever be.

She'd been too hard on him for sure. Her insistence in doing a live broadcast from the mining site had endangered Adrian's and Miguel's lives as well as her own. She couldn't have lived with herself if something had happened to them.

Which must be exactly how Neil felt about Lynne.

Carolina wanted to thump herself in the head with the heel of her hand. Honestly, how shortsighted could she be? The line between caring and controlling wasn't nearly as tenuous as she'd thought.

"Carolina!" Vi complained. "Eat."

"Okay, okay."

Without warning, the noise level in the dining room dropped to near silence. Carolina's heart began to flutter in fear. She clutched the edge of the table and automatically looked around to see what had caused the disturbance. The answer was obvious.

Neil stood near the entrance. Tall, strong and in full uniform, he made an impressive image.

Carolina couldn't believe how much safer just seeing him made her feel. No shooters would dare lurk behind a dark corner with him there.

He removed his aviator sunglasses and scanned the dining room. She sat up straighter, resisting the urge to wave girlishly. She needn't have worried. His instincts were right on target. Diners scrambled to clear a path as he came over.

"Good afternoon, ladies," he said, touching the brim of his cowboy hat when he reached Carolina's table.

"Hi." She couldn't believe how soft and shaky her voice came out. "These are my sisters, Vi, Corrine and Rachel." She pointed to each of them. "And this is Neil. Sheriff Lovitt," she added, upon seeing her sisters' conspiratorial grins.

"Nice to meet you," Vi said, "but I have to go."

"Yeah, we're needed in the kitchen to…to…take out the garbage," Rachel added.

Corrine's lame excuse followed the others.

"Please don't leave on my account," Neil said smoothly, and turned to Carolina. "Can we chat for a few minutes? Somewhere else besides here? That is, if you're done eating."

"I am." Carolina stood and together they left the dining hall. She was certain every pair of eyes in the room was fastened on them.

Outside, he surprised her by taking her hand. His fingers felt warm and firm and magically chased away the nervousness that had plagued her since the previous evening.

"Would you mind walking a bit?" he asked, something not quite right in his voice.

So much for alleviating her nervousness. "There's a foot trail that runs along the creek," she said. "It starts there, on the other side of the parking lot."

They walked in relative silence, though it was anything but silent around them. Guests were everywhere. Strolling to and from the dining hall. Swimming in the heated pool. Playing horseshoes or badminton. Riding horses or ATVs up and down the main road.

The atmosphere changed upon entering the wooded area and the trailhead. As if a thick curtain had fallen around them, Carolina and Neil were thrust into a serene calm that was broken only by the distant ruckus of children playing.

"How are you doing today?"

"Good." Her laugh came out with a slightly desperate edge to it. "I've been spending the morning trying to figure out how I can work all this into my next report."

He dropped her hand. Not a good sign.

They came to a more secluded area with a small bridge. Beneath it, the creek babbled as it rushed over rocks and around bends. Neil made no move to cross the bridge.

"I called Zoey's grandparents this morning, my former in-laws." He appeared to choose his words carefully. "She stayed with them the year after Lynne died."

"I remember you telling me."

"They're coming out for a visit in a few days."

"How nice. Zoey will be thrilled."

No answer.

Carolina began to worry in earnest. "How long are they staying?"

"A few days. Bud has to get back to work."

"That's a shame for them to come all the way from upstate New York and not stay longer. They don't get to see Zoey often."

"They're taking her back with them."

"Oh!" That was unexpected.

"She's safer with them."

"After yesterday, I don't blame you for being cautious. But sending her away seems a bit extreme."

"It wasn't a random shooting."

"I know that."

"Next time, the shooter may not miss."

"Trust me, I'm not going to the mine again."

"Damn straight you're not. If I have to tie you to your desk chair, I will."

He probably meant that in a caring way, but for some reason, his tone rubbed Carolina the wrong way. "I'm not that crazy to put myself in danger again."

"What makes you think they were after you?"

"I'm...I'm the reporter on the story."

"And I'm heading up the investigation for the department. You may not think Zoey's life is in danger, but I do."

Carolina hadn't thought of it that way.

Dear Lord, the situation had spiraled so far out of control. As soon as she got home, she was going to call Ward and remove herself from the story. No career was worth risking people's lives.

Hadn't Neil told her that very thing time and again?

"How does Zoey feel about going away with her grandparents?"

"She doesn't know, and she won't until they're ready to leave."

For a smart man, he was pretty dumb. "She won't want to go."

"She won't have a choice."

"Neil, think about this. She's not a toddler anymore. She's a bright, astute young girl who won't understand why her father's sending her away."

"I'll explain it to her."

Carolina moved to stand in front of him and placed her hands on her hips. "How are you going to do that without telling her about her mother?"

"I don't know yet."

"You could try the truth."

"She's not ready."

"Her, or you?"

"I've made my decision. Zoey will be safe. That's what matters the most."

"And two thousand miles away."

"It's temporary."

Well, at least there was a light on the horizon. By his own admission, he'd been an emotional wreck the last time he'd dispatched his daughter to live with her grandparents. Carolina would hate for him to have to go through it again. "When are you planning on bringing her home?"

"After Otis returns to work."

Two months. He could probably survive, and she would do her best to help him navigate the rough patches. But could Zoey survive without her dad?

"Or I may leave her there until I can join her."

"Join her?" Awareness stole slowly over Carolina, leaving chilly footprints up her spine. "Not bring her home?"

"I'm going to submit my resignation."

It felt like the ground shifted and rolled out from beneath her feet. Neil was leaving?

"What about us?" she asked lamely.

"I have to think of Zoey."

"Yes. Which you aren't doing and haven't from the beginning." Hurt and surprise mingled inside Carolina, giving her voice a brittle edge. "You've only been thinking of yourself and your own guilt."

"You're wrong. I'm thinking of you, too."

"Pardon me if I don't agree."

He grabbed her arm, not roughly but desperately. "You were shot at yesterday, Carolina. If you'd been hurt—killed— it would have been my fault."

"Like it was your fault Lynne died?"

"Yes."

"That was an accident."

"An avoidable one."

"You can't control everything and everybody."

"I can this. And I won't be responsible for another person losing their life on my account." He drew in a shuddering breath. "I want you, Carolina, make no mistake. But more than that, I want you alive and safe. The only way to accomplish that is for me to stay the hell away from you."

She withdrew from his grasp. "That excuse is starting to sound really tired." She knew he believed what he said, but if she heard it one more time, she'd scream. "You can't keep running away, and you can't keep sending people away. Sooner or later you're going to have to confront your problems. Only if you wait until later, your daughter may not be there. I certainly won't be."

"I was hoping you'd understand."

"You hoped I'd make it easy for you by not creating a stink."

"Trust me, you making a stink was a given."

His attempt at humor didn't amuse her. If anything, it widened the wound in her heart and caused her to strike out at him. "Can't you see what you're doing? You're so damn worried about keeping Zoey and me safe, you're losing the very thing you're trying to preserve. Our love for you."

There. She'd said it.

"I haven't lost Zoey's love. Not yet. And I don't plan to." He spoke with conviction. "Which is another reason we have to leave Payson. I can't risk her finding out about her mother."

Had he not acknowledged her admission that she loved him on purpose or had it gone unnoticed?

No, Neil wasn't obtuse.

She suddenly felt stifled by an overwhelming sense of déjà vu. Once again, she was being dumped by a man because of his job. The same feelings of hurt and rejection and anger she'd felt before came rushing back, only much stronger. Probably because they'd never entirely disappeared.

"Have it your way," she said, sniffing. "Be alone. At least you won't have to fight with your guilt anymore."

"I never wanted to hurt you, Carolina. You have to believe me."

She did. Neil's thinking might be skewed, but he'd been straight with her from the very beginning about how he felt.

She'd walked into their relationship with her eyes open. The only mistake she'd made was to think she could battle his ghosts and win.

"Contrary to popular opinion," she said, struggling to compose herself, "I won't create a stink. You'll get what you want, Neil. Your daughter will be safe, living on the other side of the country. I'll be safe, too, out of your life for good. I hope it makes you happy."

"It doesn't."

Small solace. "Then you have no one to blame but yourself." She squared her shoulders. "Forgive me if I don't walk back with you." Hell would freeze over before he saw her cry. And she would be crying. For days. "Have a good life. Wherever you wind up."

"I really wish it could have turned out differently."

She gave him one last look. "It could have."

Walking away, she decided Neil had just lost the best thing to happen to him in a long time.

But then, so had she.

So much for her life-redirecting plan.

Chapter Fifteen

"A milk truck's blocking traffic?" Rowdy Rodgers made a silly face. "I didn't think they used those anymore."

"An eighteen-wheeler hauling milk," Carolina corrected him. She wasn't in the mood to joke with the deejay. "It stalled in the middle of an intersection, and the driver can't get it started again. There's a mile-long backup, so it's best to avoid that side of town if at all possible."

"Talk about sour milk."

Rowdy frowned at her when she didn't respond to his jest and gave her a what's-up-with-you look.

She shrugged him off. "Authorities estimate another hour before traffic clears."

"Well, thanks for the update, Carolina." His inflection more than his actual words dismissed her. "I can't wait to check with you at nine."

She exited the control room a minute later. Rowdy had good reason to be annoyed with her. She'd been no more fun to work with during the four earlier reports she'd given. In fact, her entire family was fed up with her glum mood the past five days.

Carolina had neither seen nor heard from Neil since leaving him behind on the foot trail at Bear Creek Ranch. Not that she'd expected to. Once he made a commitment, he stuck to it.

Damn stubborn New Yorker. It was a shame his commitment hadn't been to resolve the issues between them.

She knew from her niece Briana that Zoey's grandparents were in town visiting, because they were picking her up from riding lessons. How long had Neil said they'd stay? A few days? Zoey would be leaving soon, possibly forever. Carolina would have liked to see her before then to say goodbye but she doubted she'd get the chance. Too bad.

For all of them.

She made her way to her private cubicle, intending to enjoy it while it lasted. Now that she'd been demoted back to morning traffic reporter, she fully expected to return to her old cubicle, the one she'd shared with the afternoon traffic reporter.

A painful lump lodged in her throat, but she didn't cry. Been there, done that, thank you.

The thing was, she missed Neil. And his daughter and the reports on the illegal mining. Other than a few scary moments—okay, hours—she hadn't felt so good, enjoyed her life so much in years.

She suspected it had been the same for him, too.

"Hey, Carolina." Ward stopped her before she entered her cubicle. "You have a minute?" He looked awful. Drawn, older. As if he hadn't slept in days.

"Sure." She changed direction and followed him, expecting to be reprimanded for not playing along with Rowdy during the broadcast. Fine. Let Ward fire her. She didn't care anymore.

A bald-faced lie, but it sounded good.

Ward led her to the conference room. Definitely a reprimand coming. He closed the door behind her, and they sat down at one end of the long table. Carolina couldn't help but recall the last time she'd been in this room. It was right after she'd received the threatening e-mail. Neil had taken her home, and they'd spent the rest of the afternoon making love.

Enough! She gave herself a stern mental kick and tried to concentrate on what Ward was saying. The poor man really did need to get some sleep before he fell apart. Even his hands were shaking.

She decided to cut him some slack. "I promise I'll joke more with Rowdy."

He gave her a blank stare. "What?"

"Rowdy," she prompted. "The traffic reports."

"I don't care about that."

"You don't?"

"I want to discuss the, uh…" He took a breath, a shallow one. "I'd like you to do a final report on the illegal mining operation."

He was just full of surprises this morning. "Why? You said yourself it was too dangerous."

"This one will be different." He spoke slowly, and his appearance became even more drawn. "The people responsible for the illegal mining will be behind bars soon."

"The authorities have caught them?" Carolina couldn't believe it.

"They're about to." His voice sounded odd.

"Ward? Are you all right?" She was really starting to worry.

"I'm very sorry you were shot at, Carolina. That was never the plan. Never what I agreed to."

"What are you talking about?" A sick, scary feeling formed in the pit of her stomach.

"Last May, my son, Len, was driving home from his senior prom. He'd been drinking. Pretty heavily."

"I don't understand what your son has to do with any of this."

"It all started with him and that night." The battle waging

inside Ward was evident on his face. "Len didn't normally drink, but you know seniors and prom night. Sheriff Herberger was coming back from a call. He's a big supporter of the school's football program. He recognized Len and pulled him over. At the time, I thought it was the luckiest break in the world."

"How so?"

"He could have given Len a DUI and hauled him to jail. He certainly deserved it—the kid broke the law. If Sheriff Herberger had, chances are Len would have lost his scholarship to ASU. Instead, the sheriff called me to come pick up Len and never reported the incident."

"That was nice of him." Carolina knew from her own experience as an occasionally wayward youth that the sheriff had a soft spot when it came to children and teenagers. Maybe because he and his wife Patty weren't able to have any of their own.

"I told him if he ever needed anything, anything at all, he had only to ask me." Ward cleared his throat. "I had no idea at the time what such an open-ended promise would cost me. What it might cost other people."

Carolina shook her head. None of this made sense.

"Sheriff Herberger contacted me when he was still in the hospital after his heart attack," Ward said. "He told me he was collecting on my debt. I couldn't say no. Not after what he'd done for Len. And, at first, what he asked for wasn't so bad."

"Which was...?"

"Apply pressure to Neil Lovitt. Attempt to discredit him by doing a story on his involvement in his late wife's death."

"Why?"

"To distract him."

"From what?"

"Investigating the illegal mining operation on your family's ranch."

"I'm confused."

"Sheriff Herberger's involved."

"You can't be serious!"

"He may even be the one behind it. I don't know everything. He intentionally kept me in the dark."

She recalled Neil's comment about the operation requiring brains and money and that the brains were local. No, it couldn't be! Sheriff Herberger was a family friend. County Sheriff for over twenty-five years.

"You're wrong."

"I wish to God I were. He knew about the mine from old maps belonging to his wife's family. He's been sneaking onto your property for the past year. He even went so far as to help an engineer from Mexico cross the border illegally. In exchange, the engineer put the crew together and oversaw the digging."

Carolina lifted trembling fingers and pressed them to her mouth. The rational part of her brain wanted to reject everything Ward said. "What about the dead phone calls and the e-mails?"

"I'm sure he's behind those, too. And the shooting at the mine site. He had contacts on both sides of the law." Ward's eyes filled with despair. "When you, Adrian and Miguel were shot at, I knew Otis had gone too far."

"I have to tell Sheriff Lovitt."

"Which is why I called you in here. I want you to break the story wide open."

"What about Len?"

"We talked for hours last night. He doesn't like this any more than I do and is ready to deal with the consequences. He feels responsible for the predicament I'm in. If he hadn't been drinking that night—"

"He didn't hire a thug to shoot at innocent people." The idea that her uncle's lifelong friend was capable of such an atrocious act horrified Carolina.

"No, he didn't," Ward said, his voice thick with regret. "He's a victim, like the rest of us. Which is why I'm telling you this now. Sheriff Herberger has got to be stopped."

"You might be arrested, too."

"At least I'll be able to sleep at night again."

Carolina appreciated the sacrifice Ward and his son were making. Confessing their involvement took courage. "I'm going to call Neil right now." She rose from the table.

"Be careful." Ward walked her to the door. "You have no idea what Sheriff Herberger is capable of, what lengths he'll go to."

Something else Neil had told her. If only she'd listened.

Still in a state of disbelief, she hurried down the hall to her cubicle. Lifting the phone, she called the sheriff's office.

"I'm sorry, ma'am," a young male voice on the other end of the line said after she'd asked for Neil. "He's not here."

"This is Carolina Sweetwater. It's very important I reach him." She almost said it was a matter of life and death. "Can you patch me through to him?"

"I'm afraid not. He's unavailable."

"Unavailable as in out of range?"

"Can someone else help you?"

"No, thank you." Hanging up, she dialed Neil's private cell phone.

He picked up on the first ring. "Carolina." It was clear he hadn't expected to hear from her.

"Neil, I have to talk to you. Right away. Can we meet someplace?"

"I can't. I'm on my way to the school. They called. There's a problem with Zoey. I don't have all the details, only that—"

"Sheriff Herberger is the one behind the illegal mining operation."

"What?" Disbelief rang in his voice.

"It's true." She talked fast, recounting what Ward had told her.

"I've got to go," Neil said tightly when she'd finished. "I'll call you later."

"Okay." She disconnected and sat there, undecided about whether to begin work on her story or phone her family. Before she could make up her mind, her cell phone rang. The caller ID flashed Neil's cell.

"Hello!"

He didn't return her greeting. "I'm en route to the Payson Police station. I've tried reaching my in-laws but they're not answering and Carmen's in class. Would you mind going to the school and checking on Zoey for me? There's no one else I trust to take care of her."

"Of course. I'll leave now." She opened her desk drawer and retrieved her purse.

"Thank you." He paused. "You have every right to tell me no after the way I've treated you."

"Zoey's more important than any argument."

When Carolina arrived at the school office, she was immediately escorted to the office where a crying Zoey was waiting. The vice principal quickly advised Carolina of what had happened. She was surprised at the trouble Zoey had gotten into—pushing and shoving another student wasn't like her—but not surprised at the reason. She'd warned Neil of this very thing.

"I don't want to go live with my grandparents," Zoey wailed, clinging to Carolina. "He can't make me."

NEIL FORCED HIMSELF to slow down as he drove the main road through Bear Creek Ranch. Though quieter than the other day, guests were still out and about, heading to their cabins as dusk faded into evening. It felt like months rather than days since he'd last been here. How would Zoey react when she saw him? How would Carolina?

He didn't deserve her kindness, not after the hurtful things he'd said to her. He'd have understood if she refused to help him. But she hadn't. She'd put her personal feelings aside for Zoey. In hindsight, he'd been right to break off with Carolina, if only because he didn't deserve her.

She'd checked in with him twice since picking Zoey up from school, informing him that she'd been in a minor playground altercation. That fact alone stunned Neil. Zoey was the shyest, most complacent child he knew. Carolina indicated there was more to what happened but refused to go into details, insisting he take care of business first, then come to her cabin to fetch Zoey.

"Business" had taken over six hours and would probably require months to wrap up completely. How long until the town recovered was another question.

Carolina and Zoey were sitting on the porch swing, bundled up in what looked like an old quilt, drinking something out of mugs. Neil guessed hot chocolate. With her many nieces around, Carolina would have that on hand. When he stepped out of the Jeep, he detected a faint aroma of food coming from inside the cabin. Whatever she'd fixed for dinner—spaghetti?—smelled good.

They watched him approach, Carolina with obvious relief and Zoey with trepidation. As he opened the gate, something small and furry sprang from the blanket, raced up the fieldstone walkway and greeted him.

If gnawing on his bootlaces could be considered a greeting.

"Where did you come from?"

The little dog yipped loudly. No, not a little dog. A puppy.

With oversize paws and ears and a tail that wouldn't stop wagging.

"Spike, down." Carolina stood, pushing the quilt over Zoey.

Neil kept walking. The puppy refused to let go. Growling, it hung on to his laces with sharp little teeth. "You went dog shopping."

"Seemed like a good idea."

"Spike?"

"I wanted to give him a tough name to grow into."

"I can see the killer instinct already."

The puppy stopped chewing and gazed up at his new owner adoringly.

"Zoey helped me pick him out."

In response, his daughter clapped and called, "Here, Spike." The puppy spun around so quickly, he lost his balance, then raced back up the porch steps to leap into Zoey's arms. She gathered him to her chest, nearly crushing him in the process.

Separating them was going to prove difficult.

"Is everything okay?" Carolina asked.

"Ward was brought into the station." Neil spoke softly so Zoey didn't hear. "Based on his statement, Otis was arrested."

"I'm sorry."

They all were. "He's refusing to talk, even with his attorney present."

"What will happen to him?"

"He'll strike a deal, eventually. Name his accomplices. His wife's apparently involved."

"Patty!"

"When she heard about Otis's arrest, she turned herself in." Neil was still trying to wrap his mind around that.

"I'll go inside and set the table," Carolina said, "so you and Zoey can talk."

"I'd rather you stayed."

"Seriously?" She seemed to be asking more than the obvious question.

He hoped his reply conveyed more than the obvious answer. "Yes."

Zoey, with Spike in tow, scooted to the far end of the swing. Neil sat down. The chains holding the swing creaked under his added weight.

"You want to tell me what happened at school today?" From the corner of his eye, Neil saw Carolina retreat to a dark corner of the porch.

"I pushed Hayden down on the sidewalk."

"Why?"

Spike offered his support by raining dog kisses all over Zoey's face.

"Cuz he's a brat and said mean things to me."

More taunts about him shooting Lynne? Poor Zoey.

"Even so, you shouldn't have done it." He might be sheriff, but apparently his daughter felt entitled to take the law into her own hands.

All at once, she started to sob. "I don't want to go away with Grandma and Grandpa."

Okay, that came from left field. "Who told you?"

"Grandma. She said I had to start packing when I got home from school today."

Damn. He wished his mother-in-law had waited for him to break the news to Zoey. Well, nothing he could do to change that now. He tried for a positive slant.

"You always like visiting them."

She flung herself at him, trapping Spike between them. "I don't want to go."

"Is that why you pushed Hayden down?"

"He told me good riddance to bad rubbish." Zoey raised a woeful expression to him. "What's rubbish?"

"Nothing you have to worry about." He stroked her hair and patted her back until she stopped crying.

"I like it here," she said around a hiccup after her crying ceased. "I don't want to move."

How did she know his plans? More grandparent interference? "I like it here, too."

"Then let's stay."

"It's not that simple."

"Grandpa says moving isn't the..." She scrunched her mouth to one side. "The slu-tion to everything."

He needed to speak to his in-laws about what they discussed with Zoey. "It isn't. I just want to keep you safe." And other people safe. "My job is dangerous."

"Carolina says you caught the bad guys."

Was *everyone* having conversations with his daughter now? Conversations, he realized, he should be having with her himself.

"The bad guys aren't all caught, but they will be soon."

"Then we can stay," Zoey announced happily.

"Oh, sweetie." He hugged her again, tighter this time.

"I don't believe you shot my mommy."

"Were the kids at school teasing you again?"

"Yes."

"Well, if we move, they won't anymore." Until someone else found out about Lynne.

"What happened to my mommy? How did she die?"

"I told you. It was an accident."

"Were you there?"

"Yes."

"Was I there?"

He glanced over at Carolina. She leaned against the railing, all but her face hidden by shadows. He didn't know it was possible, but the love and devotion shining in her eyes changed his entire way of thinking in the span of a single heartbeat.

He didn't want to leave, either. If he were honest with himself, he'd admit that what he longed for most was a permanent home. A caring wife, one who both delighted him and drove him nuts. Another kid or two. To be sheriff, a job he'd be damn good at. And, okay, it was true, a dog. Preferably one that didn't chew on the end of quilts or drink out of mugs.

If he looked around him right now, all those things were within easy reach. He just had to let go of the past and embrace the future.

It wasn't nearly as hard as he'd imagined.

"Yes, Zoey, you were there. You were just a baby, sitting in your stroller. You, your mommy and I were having breakfast at an outdoor deli."

"What's a deli?"

He looked over again at Carolina, who encouraged him with a gentle smile. As he told Zoey in simple terms what had happened the day her mother died, Carolina wiped away tears with the sleeve of her sweatshirt. Neil felt each tear as, one by one, his burden was lifted.

When he finished, Zoey raised herself up on her knees and wrapped her small arms around him. "Don't feel bad, Daddy. It wasn't your fault."

For the first time, he believed it.

She pulled back, patted his cheek, then kissed it. "I love you."

With those three words, Neil's fears, carried for four long years, dissolved. His daughter didn't hate him or blame him for her mother's death. She'd demonstrated a capacity for compassion well beyond her tender years and understood his feelings of guilt better than anyone except...

Boy, when he was wrong about something, he was really wrong.

He got to his feet, Zoey clinging to his side. Carolina had accused him of being a man of action and few words. He hoped his actions spoke for him now. Raising his free arm, he held it out to her.

Fortunately for him, she was good at reading nuances.

Catching her as she flung herself at him, he lifted her onto her tiptoes in order to kiss the socks off her.

Spike tried to get in on the act by jumping up on Neil's leg.

"Zoey and I have decided to stay," he told Carolina, his arm fitting snugly around her waist. Now that he had her, she wasn't going anywhere.

"Is that a proposal?"

He laughed. Subtlety wasn't her style.

"I'd get down on one knee but the dog's in the way."

"The answer's yes!" She gave him a smacking kiss on the lips. "Yes, yes, yes." Abruptly sobering, she pulled away. "That is, if Zoey's okay with it."

They both looked down. Zoey had picked the puppy up off the floor.

"Does this mean Spike gets to be my dog, too?"

"Absolutely." Carolina radiated happiness. "Are you up to training him?"

"Yes, yes, yes," she mimicked Carolina and twirled the puppy in a circle.

Neil thought that seemed like a good idea and did the same to Carolina. "I love you, Carolina Sweetwater."

Her laughter was like a balm, repairing the last tear in his damaged heart. Good. He wanted to be whole and new for her and his daughter and the life they would all share together.

Epilogue

The sound of squealing tires and spitting gravel rendered nearly every one of the thirty-eight happy and raucous wedding guests silent—for maybe twenty seconds. When it was obvious no one was hurt, the celebrating started up again.

So did Carolina's heart. It was her PT Cruiser, now decorated with balloons, paper flowers, streamers and "Just Married" penned with white shoe polish in the rear window that had barely missed being in another parking lot fender bender. And the driver was none other than Briana. Would her niece ever learn to be more careful?

Neil had wanted to drive the department's old Jeep to the resort outside of Payson where they would spend the night before leaving tomorrow to catch a flight to Lake Tahoe and the condo they'd rented for a week of skiing—Neil knew how, Carolina was going to learn. They also planned to do a lot of snuggling together on the living room floor in front of a roaring fire. Preferably naked. Well, it was their honeymoon, after all.

"Hello, Mrs. Lovitt." Neil drew her away from the crowd and into his warm embrace. "Or are you keeping your maiden name now that you're famous?"

"I'm not famous," she joked back. "Not outside of Payson."

"It's only a matter of time."

He could be right. Being the one to break the story about Sheriff Herberger and the illegal mining had given Carolina's career a tremendous boost. She had Ward to thank for that.

Too bad she couldn't do it in person. After cutting a deal with the prosecutor in which he was given a significant reduction in charges in exchange for his testimony, Ward and his wife quietly left Payson and relocated to Tempe, where they would be closer to his son. Ward had used the very last of his pull at the station to make sure Carolina was given the position of roving reporter.

Until yesterday morning, she'd thought that was the best possible news. Then the home pregnancy test she'd taken came back positive. Neil still didn't know. She was planning on telling him during one of those evenings spent cuddling on the floor in front of the fire. If she could hold out that long.

She brushed a tiny speck of lint off his lapel and straightened his red rose boutonniere. "You look good, Sheriff Lovitt."

They'd opted for a small, simple wedding with Neil wearing his dress uniform.

"Acting Sheriff Lovitt," he corrected her.

"Not for long."

"I have to win the election first."

"You will." She had no doubt.

Shortly after Sheriff Herberger was arrested, he was removed from office. Sadly, his health took a turn for the worse. The last Carolina had heard, he was in the hospital again, his trial postponed. Justice would eventually be served, but it saddened her that someone who had once been a pillar of the community and a close family friend had fallen so far.

Greed did that to people, she supposed—and resentment. After serving in the department over a quarter century, he'd had only his pension to show for it. Deciding that wasn't enough, he'd chosen to supplement his retirement income with illegally obtained gold after discovering a map to the mine in his wife's family heirlooms.

He should have hired a more qualified expert to check out the mine before assuming a life of crime. He would have saved himself a lot of time and money and possibly years in prison.

The reports from the Arizona Geological Society were conclusive: there would be no historic gold strike on Bear Creek Ranch. The only wealth to be made from the illegal mining operation was the fifteen percent increase in revenue as tourists flocked to the ranch's newest attraction. To mark the grand opening of the mine site, Carolina would be doing a live broadcast on location shortly after returning from her honeymoon with Neil.

He'd promised to be there. As he'd promised to stand beside her for the rest of their lives in the vows they'd recently exchanged.

"I'm going to miss you, Daddy." Zoey grabbed Neil's much bigger hand in her small one. "Hurry home."

"I'm going to miss you, too, pumpkin pie. Be good for your uncle Jake." His voice was husky with emotion.

"I will."

She and Spike were staying with Jake, his wife and his four daughters for the week. Carolina could only imagine how chaotic their house would be—and how full of love.

It was how she wanted their life to be, too. And after seeing the pregnancy test results, she was certain it would be.

Neil released Zoey, but instead of running off, the little girl turned to Carolina. "I'm going to miss you, too."

"Same here, kiddo." She bent down and gave Zoey a kiss on the cheek.

When she attempted to straighten, Zoey held on to her and whispered, "Do you think Daddy would mind if I called you Mommy?"

Carolina's heart melted on the spot. "I don't know. Why don't you ask him?"

Talk about a wonderful wedding gift!

"I will," Zoey said shyly. "When you get back."

"Okay."

"What was that about?" Neil asked when Zoey joined her new cousins for yet another photo op.

"Something between Zoey and me. She'll tell you later."

"Come on." He took her arm. "It's time to go."

"What's the rush?"

"I want to get you alone."

Neil was indeed a man of action, as he'd proved many times. And right now, what his eyes said to her was infinitely sexier than the few words he'd uttered.

Darting through a shower of bird seed, they waved goodbye to their family and friends. Rather than get in the passenger side of her PT Cruiser, she snatched the keys from his hands, sauntered around the front of the car and, shoving her long train aside, slid in behind the steering wheel.

"I'll drive."

Wearing a dumbfounded expression, he climbed in beside her.

Carolina smiled. Men like Neil needed to be shaken up every once in a while, and she intended to do just that for the next fifty or sixty years.

Harlequin offers a romance for every mood!
See below for a sneak peek from our suspense romance line
Silhouette® Romantic Suspense.
Introducing HER HERO IN HIDING by
New York Times *bestselling author Rachel Lee.*

Kay Young returned to woozy consciousness to find that she was lying on a soft sofa beneath a heap of quilts near a cheerfully burning fire. When she tried to move, however, everything hurt, and she groaned.

At once she heard a sound, then a stranger with a hard, harsh face was squatting beside her. "Shh," he said softly. "You're safe here. I promise."

"I have to go," she said weakly, struggling against pain. "He'll find me. He can't find me."

"Easy, lady," he said quietly. "You're hurt. No one's going to find you here."

"He will," she said desperately, terror clutching at her insides. "He always finds me!"

"Easy," he said again. "There's a blizzard outside. No one's getting here tonight, not even the doctor. I know, because I tried."

"Doctor? I don't need a doctor! I've got to get away."

"There's nowhere to go tonight," he said levelly. "And if I thought you could stand, I'd take you to a window and show you."

But even as she tried once more to pull away the quilts, she remembered something else: this man had been gentle when he'd found her beside the road, even when she had kicked and clawed. He hadn't hurt her.

Terror receded just a bit. She looked at him and detected signs of true concern there.

The terror eased another notch and she let her head sag on the pillow. "He always finds me," she whispered.

"Not here. Not tonight. That much I can guarantee."

Will Kay's mysterious rescuer protect her from her worst fears?
Find out in HER HERO IN HIDING
by New York Times *bestselling author Rachel Lee.*
Available June 2010,
only from Silhouette® Romantic Suspense.

HARLEQUIN® *Romance*®

GIRLS' *Weekend in* VEGAS

Four friends, four dream weddings!

On a girly weekend in Las Vegas, best friends Alex, Molly, Serena and Jayne are supposed to just have fun and forget men, but they end up meeting their perfect matches! Will the love they find in Vegas stay in Vegas?

Find out in this sassy, fun and wildly romantic miniseries all about love and friendship!

Saving Cinderella! by MYRNA MACKENZIE
Available June

Vegas Pregnancy Surprise by SHIRLEY JUMP
Available July

Inconveniently Wed! by JACKIE BRAUN
Available August

Wedding Date with the Best Man
by MELISSA MCCLONE
Available September

Silhouette Desire

From *USA TODAY* bestselling author

LEANNE BANKS

CEO'S EXPECTANT SECRETARY

Elle Linton is hiding more than just her affair
with her boss Brock Maddox. And she's
terrifed that if their secret turns public her
mother's life may be put at risk. When she
unexpectedly becomes pregnant she's forced
to make a decision. Will she be able to save
her relationship and her mother's life?

Available June
wherever books are sold.

Always Powerful, Passionate and Provocative.

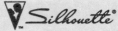

REQUEST YOUR FREE BOOKS!
2 FREE NOVELS PLUS 2 FREE GIFTS!

Love, Home & Happiness!

HAR10R

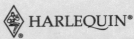

HARLEQUIN®

American ★ Romance®

The Best Man in Texas
TANYA MICHAELS

Brooke Nichols—soon to be Brooke Baker—
hates surprises. Growing up in an unstable
environment, she's happy to be putting down
roots with her safe, steady fiancé. Then she meets
his best friend, Jake McBride, a firefighter and
former soldier who's raw, unpredictable and
passionate. With his spontaneous streak and
dangerous career, Jake is everything Brooke is
trying to avoid…so why is it so hard to resist him?

Available June
wherever books are sold.

"LOVE, HOME & HAPPINESS"

www.eHarlequin.com

HAR75315

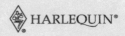

HARLEQUIN®

Showcase

Vicki Lewis Thompson

On sale May 11, 2010

Reader favorites from the most talented voices in romance

Save $1.00 on the purchase of 1 or more Harlequin® Showcase books.

SAVE $1.00

on the purchase of 1 or more Harlequin® Showcase books.

Coupon expires Oct 31, 2010. Redeemable at participating retail outlets.
Limit one coupon per purchase. Valid in the U.S.A. and Canada only.

52609015

5 65373 00076 2   (8100)0 11651

Canadian Retailers: Harlequin Enterprises Limited will pay the face value of this coupon plus 10.25¢ if submitted by customer for this product only. Any other use constitutes fraud. Coupon is nonassignable. Void if taxed, prohibited or restricted by law. Consumer must pay any government taxes. Void if copied. Nielsen Clearing House ("NCH") customers submit coupons and proof of sales to Harlequin Enterprises Limited, P.O. Box 3000, Saint John, NB E2L 4L3, Canada. Non-NCH retailer—for reimbursement submit coupons and proof of sales directly to Harlequin Enterprises Limited, Retail Marketing Department, 225 Duncan Mill Rd., Don Mills, ON M3B 3K9, Canada.

U.S. Retailers: Harlequin Enterprises Limited will pay the face value of this coupon plus 8¢ if submitted by customer for this product only. Any other use constitutes fraud. Coupon is nonassignable. Void if taxed, prohibited or restricted by law. Consumer must pay any government taxes. Void if copied. For reimbursement submit coupons and proof of sales directly to Harlequin Enterprises Limited, P.O. Box 880478, El Paso, TX 88588-0478, U.S.A. Cash value 1/100 cents.

® and TM are trademarks owned and used by the trademark owner and/or its licensee.
© 2009 Harlequin Enterprises Limited   HSCCOUP0410

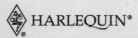

HARLEQUIN®

American ★ Romance®

COMING NEXT MONTH

Available June 8, 2010

#1309 THE SHERIFF AND THE BABY
Babies & Bachelors USA
C.C. Coburn

#1310 WALKER: THE RODEO LEGEND
The Codys: The First Family of Rodeo
Rebecca Winters

#1311 THE BEST MAN IN TEXAS
Tanya Michaels

#1312 SECOND CHANCE HERO
Shelley Galloway

www.eHarlequin.com